She Looked Up And Saw His Smile.

It should carry a mental health warning: one glimpse and you'll forget your own will. She held frantically to hers. "You said one dance and then I was free to go." Yet she left her hand on his shoulder.

"And you are free to go. But you'd rather stay and dance with me."

She met his gaze, looked into eyes that were the green of a forest river, and for a moment everything within her stilled in a kind of recognition. She struggled to recall what he'd said, struggled to hold on to her own sense of who and where she was. "That's quite an ego you have there," she said with a lightness she didn't feel.

"Perhaps." The smile left his lips but it lingered in his eyes, sought a response in hers. "Am I wrong about you wanting this next dance?"

"No."

Dear Reader,

Welcome to this, my very first Desire book.

Callie and Nick's story came to me as I played around with the idea of a hardworking "good girl" who, just once, ignores her master plan and acts on impulse—with far-reaching repercussions. Nick, another of life's planners (and whose plans definitely didn't include fatherhood), seemed like the perfect hero for her. It just took the two of them a little while to figure that out.

I've occasionally heard the process of writing a book compared to having a baby. At first there's the merest glimmer of an idea, the almost impossibility of it ever becoming anything, then the gestation period where it grows and develops, and then finally, all going well, you get to hold your baby in your arms, or hands, as the case may be.

This book is the end result of that very first glimmer of an idea and I hope you enjoy reading it even half as much as I enjoyed writing it.

Happy reading,

Sandra

SANDRA HYATT

HAVING THE BILLIONAIRE'S BABY

Published by Silhouette Books
America's Publisher of Contemporary Romance

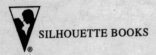 **SILHOUETTE BOOKS**

ISBN-13: 978-0-373-76956-8

Recycling programs for this product may not exist in your area.

HAVING THE BILLIONAIRE'S BABY

Visit Silhouette Books at www.eHarlequin.com

Printed in U.S.A.

SANDRA HYATT

After completing a business degree, traveling and then settling into a career in marketing, Sandra Hyatt was relieved to experience one of life's "Eureka!" moments while on maternity leave when she discovered that writing books, although a lot slower, was just as much fun as reading them.

She knows life doesn't always hand out happy endings and figures that's why books ought to. She loves being along for the journey with her characters as they work around, over and through the obstacles standing in their way.

Sandra has lived in both the U.S. and England and currently lives near the coast in New Zealand with her high-school sweetheart and their two children.

You can visit her at www.sandrahyatt.com.

For Scott.
For everything and for always.

One

Life is too short for this. Callie Jamieson stepped onto the dimly lit balcony and let the plate glass door swing closed behind her, gladly trading the glitz of the New Year's Eve wedding reception for the silent reflection of lights on Sydney's Darling Harbor.

Relaxing her grip on her champagne flute, she moved away from the pulsing beat of the music to the shadowy corner that offered not only the most privacy, but the best view of the glistening water. She shook her head and allowed herself a smile. What had she been trying to prove? The exercise regime, the new dress, new hairstyle. And at the end of it all she'd rather be walking barefoot along the water's edge. Alone.

She made her resolution then and there. Stop searching for a future or wallowing in the mistakes of her past, and start enjoying the present.

The music washed louder over her and she tensed with the knowledge that someone else had come onto the balcony. She stayed still, facing the water, hoping that the night and the slender potted palms positioned in front of the handrail would screen her from the casual observer.

"Rosa wanted me to call." A deep, resonant voice carried to her. "She insisted I do it right now. So, how's it going?" There was a long pause. "Congratulations. I guess we really do have to excuse you for not making it to the wedding." Did she imagine the catch of emotion in that warm voice? Curiosity got the better of her and Callie turned her head. A man stood midway along the balcony. With the light behind him, the only thing she could be sure of was that he was tall and that his crisply cut dark hair had a hint of a wave. With one hand he held a phone to his ear, and in his other he carried a glass of champagne the match of hers.

"Give me the details so I can pass them on to the family. We'll do the cigars when we get back." His accent was predominantly Australian, but with an underlying hint of something more exotic.

Callie glanced from her unknown companion to the balcony door and back again. Hopefully, he'd finish his call and be the one to go. She just needed a little peace, a little space before she reentered the fray and then made a discreet exit from this entire fiasco. Tomorrow morning she would be on the plane back home to New Zealand.

"Give Lisa our love." From the corner of her eye, Callie saw him start toward the door. A sigh of relief welled within her, but was cut short at the ringing of his phone.

"Nick speaking."

Nick? Brusque. Strong.

"What is it, Angelina?" The warmth she'd heard

earlier was gone. His deep, measured voice was resigned and somewhat displeased. The contrast intrigued her, and Callie turned a little more. He'd stopped partway toward the doors, and the light spilling onto him revealed broad shoulders tapering to lean hips. In the stark lines of his profile—the strong jaw, the nose with the slight bump midway along—she recognized one of the groomsmen.

There had been plenty of time during the hour-long service to contemplate the bridal party: the striking, petite blond bride, the five rose-pink, ruffled and frilled bridesmaids and the equal number of groomsmen, most of them dark-haired, and all of them good-looking.

This one's mix of careless elegance and intensity had piqued her curiosity. Was he naturally serious, did he have a problem with the wedding, or would he, like her, just rather be somewhere else?

During the second scriptural reading she had imagined a moment's eye contact, as though he'd sensed her study of him, and her mouth had run dry. Logic told her that, from her position at the rear of the cathedral, that sensation of connection, of heat, was surely impossible.

Now, as she had then, she looked away. He wasn't a friend of Jason, the groom, so his link had to be with the bride.

"You ended it, Angelina, and it was the right decision. I hadn't realized how much your expectations had changed." It wasn't as easy to stop listening as it was to stop looking. There was a long pause before he spoke again. "We agreed at the start that neither of us was looking for that sort of commitment."

Callie focused on the city lights, and though she knew she shouldn't be eavesdropping, still, a part of her waited for him to speak again. There was another even longer pause. "I'm sorry." His voice had gentled. "But no. You know this is for the best." With a heavy sigh he snapped his phone shut. "Damn," he said quietly into the night.

Callie felt for the unknown woman. She had done her time with a man who didn't want to commit. She knew the pain and sense of inadequacy that brought. She wouldn't ever go there again.

Today, she had watched the man she once thought she would marry pledge his love to another woman.

She glanced over her shoulder, and between the arching fronds of a palm saw Nick rest his forearms on the balcony railing. A warm breeze sifted through her hair. It was no hardship to wait him out. Taking a sip of chilled champagne, she looked back at the play of lights on the ink-black water. For long, restful minutes she considered how she could re-create the effect with oils.

"Solitude is one thing and loneliness another. Which is it for you?"

The words were so quietly spoken, Callie wasn't sure they were directed at her. She looked over to see that the stranger had turned in her direction. Dark eyes were fixed on her. But how to answer? Was this solitude or loneliness?

A phrase of her mother's popped into her head. "If you're choosing between bad company and loneliness choose the latter." Except, that wasn't quite right. The loneliness had been inside the dazzling reception, surrounded by others. Outside was the blissful solitude. Callie was suddenly struck by how insulting the remark could seem. Especially by a member of the wedding party. Her mother would have softened the remark with a toss of her head and a gurgle of throaty laughter.

Callie, who usually prided herself on being nothing like her mother, could carry off neither.

The man assessed her anew, curiosity rather than affront in his gaze. "Should I ask about the bad company or the loneliness?"

She sought to deflect that interest. Hopefully, he didn't know she was the ex-girlfriend, here only because she and Jason were determined to keep their relationship amicable. "Perhaps like you, I came out to take a phone call."

A half smile lifted one corner of his mouth and his amused gaze flicked over her, bringing a frisson of awareness as he took in the sleeveless, red sheath that skimmed her curves, finishing at her ankles. It was a dress she never would have worn if she'd still been with Jason. He preferred muted colors and conservative styles. There was no place on this dress for even the slimmest of phones, and her evening bag still lay on her seat between Jason's overly friendly uncle and his unfriendly cousin. Dark eyebrows rose appreciatively. "Technology is a marvelous thing."

She smiled reluctantly. "Or perhaps I just came out for some fresh air." Surreptitiously, she returned his assessment. The cut of his suit whispered tailor-made rather than off-the-rack. And no distortion of its classic lines betrayed the phone he'd slipped into a pocket.

"Or solitude?" he asked.

Her smile widened. "Definitely that."

Holding her gaze, he lifted his glass. The pale liquid shimmered golden in the light from inside, bubbles glinted like tiny jewels. "To solitude."

She raised her glass in return. The irony of toasting solitude with someone else wasn't lost on either of them.

He touched his glass to his lips and took a sip, and Callie watched the slide of his Adam's apple, then looked away, conscious of her awareness of him. For a time they remained silent. Out on the harbor a launch motored toward the bridge, the low murmur of its engine drifting across the water.

"So, is there someone waiting impatiently inside for your return?"

The undisguised spark of interest warmed her ego. "No." And for the first time that evening it didn't seem such a bad thing that Marc, her colleague, had bailed on her at the last minute. The guests and the bride and groom were supposed to have seen her dancing gaily with a gorgeous man. It was meant to demonstrate how well she had gotten on with her life.

"Then I propose another toast. To new beginnings, new lives. To freedom."

Is that what he felt over the end of his relationship? Callie lifted her glass. "To freedom." She tested the concept. And in saying the words she recognized the feeling that of late had been unfurling within her. They both took another sip.

"Unfortunately, however, I'm not as free as I'd wish tonight." He glanced inside. "Duty calls." In three strides he was at the door. He paused with his hand on the saucer-size silver disc that served as its handle and turned back to her. "Perhaps a dance later?"

His gaze, full of promise, held hers as she answered. "Perhaps." She got the feeling he wasn't often refused.

He smiled, teeth gleaming white in the night, his eyes reflecting the glitter of light from inside. It was the first smile she'd seen from him, and Callie revised her opinion as she gripped the railing for support. Merely intriguing when he wasn't smiling, he was knee-weakening when he was. He even had a dimple.

Just one, low on his left cheek. He probably had a litany of faults, but certainly none of them were obvious to the eye.

Nick pulled open the door and disappeared. Mesmerized, Callie watched the glass panel swing slowly shut behind him. She gave her head a quick shake, trying to dislodge the schoolgirl sensation of enchantment that had enveloped her while they'd been speaking.

Reality returned.

"Perhaps" was no commitment on either of their parts. She was free to go. She had come, seen Jason married, and felt almost nothing. Certainly no pain, only regret that they had stayed together for as long as they had. If he'd told her the truth—not that he wasn't ready to get married yet, but that he wasn't ready to marry *her*—they could have parted sooner. Six years seemed such a colossal waste.

She gave herself a few more minutes of the view and the peace, then crossed to the door. Blinking against the bright lights, she stepped inside. The high-ceilinged ballroom was hung with crystal chandeliers and brimmed with women in shimmering dresses and men in tuxedos. Laughter and music filled the air.

Callie glanced toward the dance floor in front of the head table and saw Nick expertly leading a plump woman in a waltz. Grinning, he lowered his head toward her silver curls and said something. The woman laughed and slapped his shoulder. Nick laughed back.

With an unexpected twinge of regret that she would never know what it was like to be held in his arms, Callie sought the exit. The doors beckoned on the far side of the room. Surely no one would either notice or care if she left now. Tonight, thoughts were turned to celebration and new beginnings. And she'd got that much herself. Closure of a chapter, a fresh page to start her life on. Tomorrow a new year would begin. She had proved, at least to herself, that she was well and truly over Jason. She wished him and Melody only the best.

She would retrieve her evening bag then slip away. But as she got closer to her table she found her way blocked by a cluster of bridesmaids, heads conspiratorially close together.

Callie tried to edge behind them, there was just enough room.

"It's not public knowledge yet," one of the bridesmaids whispered dramatically. "But Melody and Jason are both over the moon about the news. Jason hasn't stopped grinning since they found out."

Callie froze, her hips pressed against the back of a chair swathed in linen and gold.

"He's almost mollycoddling her," the whisperer continued. "Of course, she loves it."

"When's she due?" asked another.

"Six months."

Despite how much Callie wanted children, Jason had insisted that he didn't. Not yet. She had persuaded herself that she was content to wait. Obviously, his denial should also have come with the same qualification as his sentiments on marriage—*and not with you.*

Her grip on her champagne flute tightened. She had been so naive, searching for the perfect life, hoping for a future where there was never going to be one. Because, in reality she had been his holding pattern—company, while he waited for the right woman. Her chest constricted. The sensation that out on the balcony had felt like blossoming freedom withered into soggy loserdom.

She closed her eyes. She had tried so hard, and it

hadn't been enough. Taking a fortifying breath, she straightened her spine and opened her eyes. The past couldn't be changed, but the present could. She had to get out of here. She didn't even care about her evening bag. There was nothing in it she needed.

Except her room key.

Her heart sank, but she rallied. Never mind. She would go for a walk and come back for it later. With a careful sidestep, she eased herself back the way she'd come, and with escape beckoning, spun around.

And collided with Melody.

Callie's champagne coursed down the intricately beaded front of the bride's designer wedding gown.

For a second they both froze in horror. Aghast, Callie snatched up a linen napkin and blotted frantically at the dress. "Melody, I'm so sorry."

"It's okay." Melody tried to help. "It was an accident." But the bride's distress showed clearly in her wide eyes and the hitch in her breath.

Two bridesmaids rushed over looking daggers at Callie. She took a step back and was about to apologize again, when a deep voice cut through the bridesmaids' dramatic squawks. "Good thing it wasn't the merlot."

Callie looked up to see Nick rest his hand on Melody's shoulder. "It'll be okay." His quiet assurance calmed the bride, who smiled ruefully. They seemed close, and Callie wondered, not for the first time, what their connection was. She guessed Nick to be maybe a decade older than Melody's twenty-four.

"I thought it would be me who spilled the wine." Melody laughed hesitantly.

"Didn't I hear you say earlier it was time to change into your going away outfit?"

Melody nodded her agreement and was escorted away by a posse of bridesmaids, two of whom cast accusing glances back at Callie as they left.

Nick turned to her, a half smile playing about his lips. "I believe you owe me a dance."

She shook her head. "I should go."

"Why the rush? The dancing has barely begun." His large, warm hand enfolded hers, and it seemed easier to follow than to refuse him. And it was certainly easier to be in the company of someone so sure of himself. He led her between the tables, smiling and nodding at various guests, but not breaking his stride. "One dance, and then if you still insist, you can go."

They reached the parquet dance floor and he turned her into his arms. The band had begun a new song, and they waltzed effortlessly among the other couples. She remembered, almost with a start of surprise, how much she liked to dance. Jason had never enjoyed it, and so it had been a long time since she'd last felt the freedom—there was that word again—of the dance floor. Slowly the tension seeped from her. This man's presence was so potent, his touch so captivating, she could almost forget who and where she was.

He danced well, and they fit together with the ease of couples who had danced this way many times, each knowing intuitively how the other would move. The touch of his hand was firm yet gentle at her waist, his shoulder solid and powerful beneath her palm. She breathed in his scent, a mix of expensive cologne and masculinity, and smiled.

"That's better." His voice was warm and intimate in her ear.

The music slowed almost to a stop. Reality returned.

With a sense of impending loss, Callie tried to disengage her hand. The band segued into another number and Nick, his palm still curving around her waist, began moving again.

She looked up and saw his smile.

It should carry a mental health warning. One glimpse and you'll forget your own will. She held frantically to hers. "You said one dance and then I was free to go." Yet she left her hand on his shoulder.

"And you are free to go. But you'd rather stay and dance with me."

She met his gaze, looked into eyes that were the green of a forest river, and for a moment everything within her stilled in a kind of recognition. She struggled to recall what he'd said, struggled to hold on to her own sense of who and where she was. "That's quite an ego you have there," she said with a lightness she didn't feel.

"Perhaps." The smile left his lips, but it lingered in his eyes, sought a response in hers. "Am I wrong about you wanting this next dance?"

"No," she admitted, allowing her lips to curve. She was dancing with this man not because it was the appropriate or right thing to do, but purely because she wanted to. If this was freedom she could easily get used to it.

"Good."

She felt as if she'd passed some kind of test. As they glided around the floor, Callie lost awareness of everything except Nick and their bodies, of his closeness, and his supple strength. For the first time in a long time, she felt both desirable and desired. A heady sensation. And in an unsought response, she felt, too, the reciprocal stirring of yearning deep within her. She could imagine wanting more, taking more.

One dance blended into the next. The music changed to something with a slow, steady rhythm and a Latin-American feel. And as they moved. Nick looked down at her. Those river-green eyes seemed to see right into her. *Please let him not know the forbidden territory her thoughts had ranged to.* Callie looked away and was startled to realize that, save for one other couple locked in an embrace, the dance floor was now empty and the crowd in the ballroom had thinned considerably. As if in a waking dream, she looked back into Nick's eyes and felt herself drawn deeper.

His eyes darkened. With a fluid movement, he spun her away, then drew her back into him. For a second her back pressed against him, his arms encircled her. With another turn, she was facing him again and breathing more rapidly than the dancing warranted.

Her awareness centered wholly on this man and the way their bodies moved together to the rhythm of the music. He led expertly, signaling with his touch where he wanted her to go, and she followed that self-assurance effortlessly.

She thought in that moment that she, who liked to lead in life, would follow him anywhere.

They turned and for a passing moment their thighs intertwined. Loverlike. The desire that had been smoldering all evening ignited and swept through her.

"Tell me your name?" His jaw, faintly shadowed, was only a whisper away from her face, and his voice resonated through her.

"Calypso." She chose to tell him her full name. She didn't often use it. Jason had never liked it; he'd thought it odd. But wasn't tonight about reclaiming a part of herself she'd lost? She'd been named after a boat, for goodness' sake, but at least a boat that had sailed the high seas and sought adventure.

Another turn. "It's beautiful," he said. Her gaze met his, and the masks were stripped away. He saw the desire she couldn't conceal. She saw its match in the green depths of his eyes.

He wanted her.

Her pulse leapt as her mouth ran dry. She wanted him too.

The ground seemed to disappear beneath her feet, replaced by the soaring sensation of freedom. Terrifying and exhilarating. The freedom to choose—that power heady and intoxicating. Or perhaps that was the man himself. It had been so long since anyone had looked at her like that.

He exuded confidence, strength and a barely concealed sexuality. And he tempted her. But she also knew he wanted no commitment. He was not at all what she was looking for.

But searching for what she thought she wanted had resulted in disappointment and disaster. She reminded herself of her resolution to live in the present, to seize life.

Perhaps? The word shimmered with limitless possibilities. Perhaps for tonight she could throw caution and practicality and planning to the wind, and go where fate, or lust, was leading her. Perhaps for tonight she could seize life with both hands and actually live a little. Tomorrow she would return to her real life of responsibilities and careful planning. But tonight...

"Are you ready to go?"

She knew what he was asking. "Yes."

* * *

Nick held Calypso's delicate hand in his as he led her to the elevators. She asked him no questions, offered nothing about herself. That lack of any attempt to create a basis for intimacy told him she wasn't looking for any more than he was. Perhaps it was because of that reticence that he suddenly found he wanted to know more about her—who she was, what made her laugh, what made her cry, her secret hopes and fears.

His sister's wedding was the last place he thought he'd meet someone and feel this pull of attraction. After the tensions of the last few months with Angelina, both before and after their relationship ended, he'd planned on enjoying a break, some time on his own without the demands of a relationship.

The solitude he had toasted with the woman now at his side.

But there was something different about this woman. He had felt a connection the moment he'd first seen her dark silhouette in the night. He felt a connection now, just holding her hand in his.

Some things are meant to be. His grandmother Rosa's words. He tamped down on the thought. He wasn't a believer in fate. A man created his own destiny. But this…this felt like fate. He could almost hear Rosa's soft, knowing laugh. Rosa, who had sent him outside to make that call. As though she had known…something.

No matter how often he denied it, she insisted that Nick was the only one in the family to have inherited her *gift*. And sometimes, like now, he could almost believe it. He smiled when he realized what he was doing, using mumbo jumbo to justify going to bed with a woman he'd just met.

This wasn't destiny. This was his libido awakening. He pressed the button for the elevator.

"You're smiling?"

He looked down at the woman beside him and was drawn into her chocolate-colored eyes. He lifted his free hand, fingered one of the silken curls that framed her face. He could imagine how she would look the morning after a night of passion—tousled and sleepy. The thought took him by surprise. His mind didn't usually leap so far ahead with a woman. He lived moment by moment. But he could see the morning after, could imagine breakfasts in bed. Could imagine lunches, dinners, more dancing. "I have a lot to smile about."

Her own smile in return was hesitant, but no less powerful for that. Satisfaction and desire swelled. He had wanted to make her smile, to erase a shadow of sorrow that seemed to lurk behind her eyes. He knew that, for tonight at least, he could make her forget everything. A knowing glint touched her eyes and temptation leaped. He wrenched his gaze away. If he kissed those softly parted lips now he wouldn't want to stop. He jabbed the button again, and was rewarded with the ping signaling the elevator's arrival.

As the doors slid closed, secluding them in the private space, he did what he'd ached to since he first saw her standing alone on the balcony. He curved his fingers around her slender neck, his thumb resting at the softly vulnerable juncture of throat and jaw, her hair like silk cascaded over his knuckles.

Savoring the moment, he bent his head to taste her.

It was a gentle kiss, as though they had all the time in the world. She tilted her head and the kiss deepened. Peaches. She tasted of the sun-ripened peaches that had been served with dessert. Her lips were pliant beneath his. Their bodies scarcely touched, and yet need for her arrowed through him.

He was a man who stayed in control. At all times. He was known for it. But here, in an elevator, that control was perilously thin. It was with a mixture of despair and reprieve that he realized they had arrived at the top floor and the doors were waiting open.

He lifted his head, looked again into those deep brown eyes and reached for her hands. Her hastily retrieved evening bag dangled from one slender wrist as he raised her hands to his lips and kissed each of her knuckles in turn.

They walked toward his suite. It seemed important not to rush. Time needed to be taken to absorb her, the touch of her hand, the scent of her hair, the awareness of how her body moved so close to, and so in tune with his.

Pulling the card key for his room from his pocket, he hesitated as he held it above the slot. He looked at her, wanted her to be absolutely certain. Wanted to know that this craving wasn't of his own imagination. She slid the card from his fingers and inserted it. When the access light blinked green, she pushed open the door and stepped into the room ahead of him.

She turned and reached toward him. As he took her hands in his, the thought that he never wanted to release them assailed him. He met her gaze, losing himself in eyes that seemed both brazen and innocent. With a smile that matched her gaze, she pulled him through the doorway and into her arms.

For a moment she stood pressed against his chest, fitting perfectly, as he knew they would fit in other ways. Her supple warmth flowed into him, heated him further still.

She tilted her face upward and kissed him. And took his breath away.

Again that taste of peaches, and beneath that a subtle flavor and scent that was hers alone, enhanced by the heat and longing of desire. His hands skimmed over her curves, the red fabric of her dress silken and sliding beneath his palms.

He ached to claim her. Every inch of her. With every inch of him. He needed this to be as unique and special for her as every sense told him it was going to be for him.

He wanted tonight to last forever.

He broke the kiss and rested his forehead against hers. He cupped her pale shoulders bathed in the dim city light that spilled through the window. Beneath his touch he felt movement as her hands, both delicate and forceful, pulled his shirttails free, worked buttons undone until they slid—exploring, learning and trailing fire in their wake—up his front and settled on his chest, over his heart. Did she feel how it pounded with the blood that rushed through him for her?

There was a moment of stillness, the calm before the storm, and then they were kissing again, tongues teasing and dancing, that connection remaining true as clothes were peeled away and discarded.

Her beauty and her passion staggered him, stirred something unknown within him, a primal intensity that made him want to claim her not just for now, but for always.

The *now* he knew how to deal with as they fell onto his bed.

Dawn was just beginning to lighten the sky when Callie slipped from the tangle of luxurious sheets. It wasn't till she'd finished dressing that she turned back to look at Nick. Even sleeping, he enthralled her. He was…beautiful. There didn't seem any other word for it. His dark hair was tousled, eyelashes curved above high, shadowed cheekbones. One arm was thrown up above his head, the bicep pale and curving. And the chest. Ahh, the chest. Callie took a moment for that alone.

Recalling herself, she crossed to the desk in the suite, her footsteps cushioned by the deep carpet. As she looked for a pen and paper she contemplated what to say, how to say it. Name and number alone? Thank you? Something witty about his kind of company being so much better than solitude? She looked at the sleeping man again. If she leaned down and kissed those lips he'd awaken. But she had a plane to catch.

Picking up a silver pen, she reached for one of the business cards that sat in a small, neat stack. About to turn it over she glimpsed his full name.

And froze.

Dominic Brunicadi. She dropped the card as though it burned.

What had she done? The billionaire bachelor was many things—almost a client, newly related to her ex, and way, way out of her league—and all of those things precluded her having anything to do with him.

Two

Nick strode through the crowd at Auckland Airport, and despite his best efforts, thoughts of Calypso stole into his mind. The turn of her head, the light in her eyes, the delight of her laughter.

In the month since *that* night, he'd had a hard time forgetting her. There had been incredible chemistry between them, on the balcony, on the dance floor and later. He remembered it only too well, and too often. Or perhaps the plaguing sense of something lost was only pique that she had vanished.

He'd asked a couple of people who she was, but they hadn't known. He wouldn't ask more, because he liked to keep his private life just that. Still, he felt like he was trying to track down Cinderella. She must have been from Jason's side, and he fully intended asking Jason about her when the opportunity presented itself.

He had no intention of chasing after a woman who clearly wanted nothing further to do with him. She'd left no means of contacting her, nor had she called him—though he'd noticed his business cards had been disturbed. But he needed to know who she was.

And for his own peace of mind he needed to know the answer to one small but vital question.

He scanned the crowd. Ridiculous to even think he might see her here. Milling passengers riffled through bags and papers looking for passports and tickets, frazzled parents attempted to quiet fractious children. Ruthlessly, he pushed thoughts of her aside. He had his sights set on the exit doors and was mentally assessing his upcoming appointments when his cell rang. Not breaking his stride, he pulled the phone from his pocket and checked the ID.

"Melody?" He hadn't expected to hear from his sister so soon. She and Jason only got back from their honeymoon a few days ago. "How was Europe?"

He let his sister gush about their travels as he found the black Mercedes parked outside and slid into the seat.

"Glad to hear it went so well." Nick turned the key in the ignition and the engine purred to life. "But that's not why you called me, is it?" Mel seldom called without there being a reason. She knew he wasn't one for idle conversation. There was a suspiciously long pause.

"It's Jason."

Nick sat up a little straighter. Surely there wasn't trouble in paradise already. He didn't quite have Jason figured out yet, he'd spent so little time with the man. Nick had been in Europe when the relationship started, and it had progressed so rapidly that suddenly wedding invitations were going out. All he knew for sure was that Melody was besotted and she was happier than he'd seen her in years. So far, he'd been able to like the guy for that reason alone. "What's wrong?"

"Nothing. At least, I think it's nothing."

"What is it, Mel?"

He heard her indrawn breath. "I'm worried about his ex at Ivy Cottage PR."

He recognized the name of the New Zealand–based firm that Mel used for Cypress Rise, the boutique winery associated with their family home in the Hunter Valley. Mel had met Jason through his work on the winery's account. Nick knew nothing about the other partner, Jason's ex. "What about her?"

"It's probably nothing…."

"But?" Mel wouldn't be calling if she thought it was nothing.

"She and Jason used to be more than just business partners, and he still has a lot of contact with her. He wants to buy out her share of the business and run it from here, boost up the Australian side of things." Melody spoke quickly, as though unburdening herself. "He's offered her a good price, but she won't sell. He says he doesn't want to pressure her, but it's like she won't let go of him. And now she's phoning him at unusual times, late at night and early in the morning."

"Do you think you could be overreacting?" Mel had been hurt in the past and had been wary ever since.

"I could be. I probably am."

"But you're still worried?"

Melody gave an unconvincing laugh. "Yes."

"And you'd like me to go see her?"

"You're in New Zealand. And you have such a good feel for people. You could go in your capacity as a director of the winery."

"Even though I have nothing to do with the day-to-day running of the company?"

"I'd just like your opinion. I mean, she seemed nice, but most of my dealings with the business were with Jason."

Nick sighed. Melody was the only person who could twist him around her little finger. It had been that way since she came into the world ten years after him, and the bond between them had only strengthened with the death of their mother when Melody was three. Their father had coped by immersing himself in work, largely leaving the children to deal with their loss together. "I'll see if I can fit her in." They both knew that was as good as a promise. "Where do I find her?"

"Thanks." He heard the relief in her voice. "It means a lot to me."

But when he did make time to call in at the ivy-covered cottage on the outskirts of the city, Ms. Jamieson wasn't in, and the surprisingly young receptionist, with spiky, ink-black hair tipped with red, would only say she wasn't due back in the office till Monday morning.

However, what he did spy on the receptionist's desk was an invitation to an awards ceremony taking place that evening. He recalled Melody telling him earlier about the New Zealand PR campaign for their wines being nominated for an award, and how she wouldn't be able to go, because she'd only just be back from the honeymoon. He considered his evening ahead. He could reshuffle a few things.

In the glittering banquet hall, Nick talked easily to acquaintances from the hotel and wine industry as he scanned the room. Even if, as he suspected, Melody was overreacting, the evening wouldn't be a total waste of time. He'd picked up some useful pieces of information and made contact with several colleagues he hadn't seen in a while. One of them had pointed out Kelly Jamieson, seated at a table with her back to him. Glossy brown hair was pulled into an elegant twist at the back of her head. She wore a high-necked, slim-fitting gown of a dazzling electric blue. There was something familiar about the tilt of her head, and the pale creamy shoulders.

Nick blocked the thoughts and concentrated on the business at hand. All he needed was to talk to Ms. Jamieson and assess her intentions. As he started toward her, the woman turned her head and he caught a glance of her profile, long lashes, high cheekbones and a jaw with a hint of defiance.

Not Kelly, but Callie, Calypso.

He couldn't name the feeling that slammed into him. In the first unguarded instant it was almost something triumphant.

He'd found her.

But after that brief, shimmering moment, triumph turned to doubt and a sharp sense of betrayal. He paused. Relegating emotion, he sorted through the facts. This was the woman Mel suspected of interfering in her marriage. The same woman who had slept with him at Mel's wedding and then disappeared. A woman who had given him a name that, if not exactly false, didn't seem to be the name she was known by.

What if Mel's concerns weren't unfounded? What if she had slept with him to get at his sister or Jason? He had to at least consider the possibility.

Callie sat at the large round table, idly spinning the stem of her empty wineglass between thumb and fore-finger as she listened to Robert from Harvey PR explain in detail the campaign his company had been nominated for.

She tried to be attentive, but couldn't help her relief when finally the MC, a moonlighting television presenter, stood behind the podium and gradually the conversation died away. The chair on her right was pulled out and she glanced up at the tall figure beside her. As the MC began his introduction the breath stalled in her lungs.

"Nick." His name passed her lips on an exhalation that left her feeling winded.

Over the last month she'd constantly tried, and failed, to stop thinking about him. Seizing the day—or night—had seemed such a good idea at the time. And a spectacularly bad idea in the dim light of an early Sydney morning.

"Calypso." He sat easily in the chair next to her, smiled a greeting to the others at the table before turning back to her. His gaze met hers. For long seconds she could only stare. Her heart and her head vied for control of her reaction.

She looked into the green depths of his eyes and saw…nothing, not the warmth she remembered, no surprise, either. He was studying her, looking for something, but she couldn't tell what. "You left early the morning after the wedding."

Early and fast. She'd practically sprinted from the room after seeing his business card. She lifted her chin, didn't want him to see her turmoil. "I had a plane to catch."

"Of course." He agreed easily. And yet, despite the outwardly relaxed manner, she had the feeling he was anything but.

She hadn't once seen him in her three years working with the Cypress Rise account, and she'd fervently hoped that trend would continue. All she wanted was to be able to put him out of her mind. As she looked at him now, she was forced to accept that things just weren't going her way lately.

It also didn't help that for the last couple of weeks she'd been working on the Jazz and Art festival she was organizing for Cypress Rise. In fact, with the account so to the fore of her workload, she'd actually congratulated herself for pausing only occasionally to bang her head on her desk and mutter, *What was I thinking?*

She took a deep and supposedly calming breath. "I wasn't expecting to see anyone from Cypress Rise here. Melody said—"

"That she couldn't make it. Fortunately, I could."

"Fortunately." She tried and failed to imbue the word with sincerity.

His gaze flicked over her before coming back to her face. "You're looking very demure tonight." The softly spoken words contrasted dramatically with the cool gaze. "Though I think I preferred the siren-red, with the low neck and that delectable thigh-high split in the side."

This was no wistful recollection. She looked at him, confused by his thinly veiled accusation. Where was he going with this?

"And your hair. I liked it loose against your shoulders." For a moment the sharp gaze softened. "I liked the way it brushed across—"

"This is a business function." Callie said quickly before he could call to mind images that had no place here.

He straightened. "As opposed to a seduction?"

Her confusion deepened. "Surely, you're not suggesting that—"

"I'm not suggesting anything. Just curious."

"About?"

"Several things. Your name, for instance. Everybody else seems to know you by Callie."

"It's Calypso, but I don't always use the full version." Why was she feeling that she had to defend herself for using her own name?

"Ahh." The river-green eyes were narrowed. Strange how, at the wedding, those eyes had seemed full of promise and passion. If there was promise there now, it was not of good things to come.

"We'd toasted freedom." She gave in to the urge to explain. "Calypso felt right for…then."

His face advertised his disbelief. Was she being accused of both seducing and deceiving him? Callie's spine stiffened. She lowered her voice. "Over the last few weeks I've engaged in plenty of self-recrimination for my lapse in judgment that night. And though I'm happy to heap blame on myself, I'm not going to let you do it, because there were two of us in that room—equal partners." The sense of equality in itself, something she hadn't felt before in the bedroom, had been liberating. But it wasn't something she wanted to dwell on now.

A waiter came to stand at her shoulder, offering to fill her glass. She nodded acceptance, though she seldom drank. Jason and Melody's wedding being a notable exception. Still, the wine was a Cypress Rise vintage, and she'd scored something of a coup in getting it served tonight.

The MC finished a joke about the PR and advertising business and good-natured laughter filled the room. Callie hadn't heard a word of it.

Nick leaned in, his face so close she could almost count the dark, spiky lashes framing his accusing eyes.

"It's not equal if one person has far more information than the other, and if that person chooses to withhold it."

She held that gaze. To think she'd once imagined a connection with this man. The cold reality was that he was a complete stranger. "I withheld no more than you did."

"You're saying you didn't know who I was?"

She leaned in, too, matching his stance while she made her point. "Not till the next morning, when I saw your business card."

"Despite the speeches?"

A strange heat built, as neither of them backed away or broke the contact of their gaze. Callie desperately wanted to attribute the heat to anger. "Most of which I missed." To avoid Jason's uncle and his unavuncular patting of her thigh.

"I was in the wedding party."

She fought the distraction of the familiar, masculine scent of his cologne. "There being so few of you in the wedding party, and the resemblance between you and your sister being so striking." Nick, olive-skinned and over six feet tall, looked nothing like petite, blond Melody. He gave a single, slow nod of his head. He seemed to be acknowledging, if not exactly buying, her point.

"I can't think why you're so reluctant to believe me. Aside from anything else I would never have…a relationship—" what else could she call it "—of that kind with a client."

"Company policy?" he asked in a deceptively calm voice.

Given what had happened between Jason and Melody, she could hardly insist that it was. "Personal ethics," she said instead.

For long seconds he continued to study her. Finally

he looked away and relief washed through her at the break in the tension. He took a sip of his wine, savored it before swallowing. He'd heard her defense; she didn't know if he believed it.

"Look, Nick. We shared…" She broke off as a second waiter appeared and placed a plate of mango salad in front of each of them.

"Fantastic sex." He finished for her in a voice that was low, but not low enough. The waiter's eyes widened as he looked at her. Callie glared at him and he backed deferentially away.

She transferred her glare from the waiter to its rightful target, but chose to neither confirm nor deny the question. Denying it would be a blatant lie, and confirming it suddenly seemed like a very bad idea.

"A night."

He smiled at her choice of words.

"Of freedom. But…"

"But?" There was something in his eyes. A memory?

Much as she didn't want to, she remembered too. "That's all it was." She'd had her taste of that kind of freedom, and it wasn't for her. That one night had crystallized her goals and needs. Her plans for her life centered on her business and hopefully one day finding the right man, a man who appreciated the simple things in life—like love—a man who wanted to settle down and have children. Even if she hadn't heard Nick ending a relationship that was looking like too much commitment, the research she'd done on him after she came home told her not only of his phenomenal success in business— buying up companies like she bought coffees—but also of the string of glamorous women he dated.

The MC's voice broke over them as he announced the

winner of the first category. Callie applauded as Tony,
a colleague and university classmate, headed for the
stage. He made a brief speech of acceptance and thanks.

As the main course—mustard-seared rack of lamb—
was served, Callie picked up her fork and, from the corner
of her eye, watched as Nick picked up his. She saw his
hands, strong and capable, remembered what those hands
had done to her. Nick leaned closer. She caught his scent
again, and despite or perhaps because of her anger, it
stirred something else equally primal, and equally re-
sented. Because all they had shared was dancing and sex,
all her thoughts associated with him were physical and
intimate. She fought to shut down that awareness.

He nodded at her untouched wine glass. "You're
not drinking."

Again she was caught off guard by where his
thoughts might be heading. "I don't." She tried to sound
nonchalant.

"You did at the wedding."

"Not much. Mostly I just carried the glass around." As
though holding a glass could make her look like she was
having a good time. "And it's not a commandment or
anything. I make the occasional exception." Like, if she
really felt the need to fortify herself as she had that night.

Tonight, on the other hand, she got the feeling she
needed her wits about her more than anything else.

"Are you pregnant?"

Callie's fork clattered to her plate and she looked up.
A frown pleated his brow. His eyes had softened as they
searched her face. She looked away.

"Keep your voice down. It's not going to be good for
my business if the rumor starts circulating that I'm
pregnant."

The MC introduced Len Joseph, an old mentor of Callie's and an industry stalwart, who would be announcing the nominations for Innovation in a Small Business, the category she was a surprise finalist in.

"I wondered, because of—"

"I'm not." She cut him off before he could say the words "broken condom" aloud. That had been the one awful surprise in an otherwise blissful night. But it had broken early during their lovemaking, and they'd assured each other it would be okay. She closed her eyes for a few seconds. Please let this be over and then she could slip out of here and never have to see this man and all the things he reminded her of again.

"You've had your period?"

She opened her eyes and looked hastily around to make sure no one was listening in on their conversation. "Yes." She'd had her period. It had been a little late and a little light, but she'd definitely had it. "Now, could we change the subject, please?"

Some of the tension eased from Nick's jaw and shoulders. What would he do, or want to do, if she had become pregnant? He'd surely be appalled by the prospect. And she couldn't blame him. She wouldn't know what to do herself. But to get pregnant after her one and only one-night stand would have surely been both incredibly unlikely and incredibly unlucky.

And she would have had only herself to blame. She should never have acted on the compulsions of that glittering night. Besides, she'd provided the condoms. She had slipped the little box, a present from her PA, into her evening bag as she'd got ready that evening, never expecting to use them. They were a symbol of her independence, a step on her journey of liberation.

She'd decided, as she'd worried about the repercussions of what she'd done, that some kinds of liberation weren't all they were cracked up to be. What she sought lay within herself, not with someone else.

Callie turned back to her unwanted meal. And yet, there was that loudly ticking biological clock, the one that had lately started chiming the quarter hour, as well, and that little voice that, when she was least expecting it, whispered "a baby" in reverential tones. She might not know precisely what she'd do if she was pregnant, but she couldn't help sometimes wondering. After her relief at the arrival of her period there had been a quiet, fleeting disappointment.

Suddenly, Robert Harvey clapped her on the back. Applause sounded and Callie looked up to see her stunned face on the enormous screen at the front of the room.

Dammit. She'd won her category.

She dredged up a smile; but as she stood to walk to the stage, Len noticed Nick and called him to come up with her as a representative of Cypress Rise. Callie couldn't believe it. Wasn't it just her luck that the two men knew each other?

Nick's hand touched lightly at the small of her back as she climbed the stairs, and she had to fight the urge to spin around and slap it away, because even that courteous touch caused sparks of unwanted awareness.

She accepted the plaque and the asymmetrical glass award with a kiss on the cheek from Len, then turned to find Nick directly in front of her. "Congratulations," he said, and she couldn't read the expression in his eyes. Strong hands curled around her bare upper arms as he bent to kiss her briefly on one cheek. "I remember the scent of your perfume." The softly spoken words teased across her skin. "It's haunted me for the last month." He kissed her other cheek, Italian fashion. The applause increased. Fingers trailed the length of her arms as he stepped away. He was playing to the audience, the louse, and could have no idea how very much he disconcerted her.

"Touch me again after this," she said with a wide smile, knowing only he would hear her words "and I'm sure I could find a novel use for this sharp and surprisingly heavy award."

Nick's quiet laughter was low and deep and seemed to resonate at a frequency her body was attuned to, stirring…feelings. Feelings she couldn't—didn't want to name.

He stood behind her as she made a brief, impromptu acceptance speech. She could feel his presence, an aura of charisma and attraction. She hastened back down the stairs, but was stopped at the bottom by a photographer from a business publication covering the event. "Ms. Jamieson, a photo of you and your client, please? Mr. Brunicadi, could you stand a little closer?"

A flash went off as she was about to respond.

"Thanks." The man dashed off while bright spots still floated in front of her eyes.

Callie headed toward her table. The temptation to keep right on walking was fierce. She needed to get away from this man who made her think of the touch of city lights on the planes and contours of his body, who made her remember how she had been when she was with him—uninhibited, passionate—a woman she didn't quite recognize.

The real her didn't know how to handle being with Nick again. Whereas being with her didn't appear to bother him at all. Clearly, he'd had way more practice than she at seeing again someone you'd once slept with. As they neared her table, Nick slowed her with a hand on her arm. He glanced at the exit and shook his head as though he'd read her thoughts. "It'd be bad form." He pulled out her chair. "Stay. Enjoy your moment."

Callie glanced around the room—already smiling colleagues were making their way toward her. She looked back at Nick. "I'll stay because for the first time tonight you're right, it would be bad form. But you on the other hand, may as well leave, because I have nothing further to say to you."

His gaze flicked to the trophy she clutched, then back to her face. "I'll leave." He held her gaze. "Because with this win you'll be swamped for the rest of the evening. But, Calypso, we're not finished."

Three

Nick spread the morning paper out, frowning as the white wrought-iron table, too insubstantial for his liking, wobbled beneath his touch. Sunlight streamed onto the veranda of Calypso's gracious villa, promising another hot day. He leaned back in the chair and slipped on his sunglasses. It could almost be pleasant here. All he needed was a cup of good coffee. He checked his watch. Hopefully it wouldn't be too long before he could leave and get himself one.

He glanced at a vineyard not three hundred feet away. Long rows of vines stretched over the contours of the land. Even from this distance, he could see that the vines were ill-pruned and the grass around them too long.

Shaking his head, he turned his attention back to the paper. It wasn't his problem how her neighbors tended their vines. He skimmed the headlines before turning to the business pages. A photo of Calypso and him graced the second page. He studied the picture, saw her wide eyes, her full mouth, and a sensuous figure that even her seemingly modest dress couldn't disguise. Questions assailed him. Why had she really slept with him? If it was simple attraction, why had she disappeared? Why the late-night phone calls that Melody was so worried about?

They were questions he needed answered. But could he trust her? Or, more importantly, could he trust his own judgment, when every thought about her was clouded with memories, and an attraction that wouldn't abate?

He would keep her close till he had his answers, and if that closeness bothered her he'd look on it as a small measure of payback.

The bang of a cupboard door shutting sounded in the kitchen behind him. Last night he hadn't been prepared for the fact that Melody's problem woman and his mystery woman were one and the same. His resolve had been undermined by her confusion and his. And despite everything else, there had been no need to detract from her success in winning the award. She deserved that time to celebrate. So he had left.

But today was a new day and he was ready, anticipating their next clash.

A couple of minutes later the French doors at the other end of the veranda swung open and Callie stepped out. He didn't know what he'd expected, but it wasn't this.

He'd seen her in sleek red and dazzling blue, both times a mix of glamorous, elegant and sensual, but now her long legs and delicate feet were bare, she wore a white silk-and-lace negligee, but over the top of it an unbelted, soft, pink terry cloth bathrobe. The taunting contrasts of sweet innocence and seductress.

A man could slip his hands beneath that robe, cradle the silk-covered hips. He knew how her skin would feel beneath his touch. Nick swallowed, forced his gaze upward.

She held a steaming yellow mug. The scent of fresh coffee reached him. Walking to the edge of the veranda, she tipped her face up to the sun, closed her eyes and inhaled deeply.

Suddenly he wished he was anywhere but here. He didn't want to notice the rise and fall of her breasts. All he needed was answers, not to be seduced all over again. Though a part of him that wouldn't be silenced couldn't help but wishing it might be the other way around.

Callie turned and saw him and the serenity in her face transformed to shock. "What are you doing out here?"

"I didn't think you'd want me coming inside before you were up."

A frown drew her brows together. "I don't want you coming inside at all."

"It's a good thing I'm out here then, isn't it?" His deliberate calmness was a counterpoint to her flustered outrage. He'd discomposed the cool, Calypso Jamieson of last night. He knew better than to let his satisfaction show—or the fact that she discomposed him equally.

"No! It's not a good thing. I told you last night that I had nothing further to say to you." Her wide brown eyes flashed fire.

"You did. But though you may not have wanted to continue our conversation, I still have questions. And I want answers."

Callie strode the few steps to the table and set her mug down. Hot liquid slopped over the side.

With a touch of his fingers, Nick shifted the newspaper out of the way of the spreading puddle. "Mind your paper. Though, given your penchant for spilling drinks, I suppose I should be grateful I'm not wearing that."

"Given my feelings on finding you here at all, you should definitely be glad you're not wearing it." Her frown deepened. "Whose paper?"

He shrugged. "It was down by the mailbox. I brought it up for you."

"Make yourself at home, won't you." Color suffused her face and her deceptively sweet voice was heavy with sarcasm. "Can I get you a drink? A cup of coffee? Perhaps you'd like a bagel?"

Nick glanced at her coffee, then the damp patch on the table. "No, thanks."

It might be pushing her too far to take her up on her offer, though it would almost be worth it to see her reaction.

He wanted to rile her, to unsettle her as she had him, as her proximity continued to do. But that wasn't what he was here for, and he needed to remember that. He closed the paper and folded it in half, pushing it to one side. "Why won't you sell your share of Ivy Cottage PR to Jason?"

Those brown eyes widened. "What?"

"You heard me."

"Yes, I heard you, but I can't quite believe the question."

"Believe it."

Her hands clenched into fists at her sides. "What I do with *my* business is just that, my business, not yours. I suggest you stop wasting your time, and mine, and leave."

He folded his arms. "I'm making it my business, and

I'm not going anywhere till I have some answers. We can get this over and done with through this one, simple conversation, or we can drag it out as long as you like. The choice is yours."

Her fists stayed clenched, but she shifted them to her hips. "What I want is for you to go. Leave, please. Now."

He didn't have time to be curious, but he didn't think anyone had ever tried to order him from a premises before. Nick slid his sunglasses from his eyes so he could meet her gaze directly. He wanted her to see just how serious he was. "I'm booked on a flight back to Sydney this afternoon. I'd like to catch it. Answer a few questions and I will. Choose not to answer and I'll be in your office on Monday morning, and then Tuesday and Wednesday.... You get the picture."

She didn't answer.

"Of course you can still refuse to speak to me, even at your office, but with you being the PR expert, you can imagine what the press would make of a rift between your firm and the client you've just won an award for. Quite an interesting tidbit. They do so love those stories with a human interest angle."

She stared at him and the silence lengthened. He didn't mind. He was good at silences.

"I'm getting changed." She stalked away.

Nick took her response as a concession. She would be coming back. He spread out the paper again and wondered if she'd make him wait endlessly. But she returned quickly. So at least she wasn't playing games. She wore slim-fitting jeans and a snug white T-shirt. Thankfully, now his focus wouldn't be splintered by expanses of creamy skin. Although her curves beneath the worn denim and soft cotton were their own definition of temptation. He focused on her face. It was just as bewitching. Only the righteous anger in her eyes helped ground him.

"I'm starting to see a picture," she said, her head tilted to one side. "Last night's insinuation of seduction and deception, this morning's ill-founded accusations." She pulled out the chair opposite him and sat down. "This has something to do with Jason and your sister, hasn't it?"

"You tell me. Explain the late-night phone calls, explain your reluctance to sell."

She continued studying him, but didn't answer his questions. "You were very quick to believe I had an ulterior motive in sleeping with you." Humor suddenly danced in her eyes. "Do women usually need one?"

He suppressed the smile that threatened. "It's not been my experience." He turned the tables back on Callie. "So you're saying it was attraction, pure and simple?"

Her eyes widened as she realized the trap she'd fallen into. "A *passing* attraction," she said quickly.

This time he let his smile show. Because, despite what either of them said, the attraction was still there, sizzling in the air between them.

She looked away. He used the opportunity to study the curve of her neck exposed by the ponytail she'd pulled her hair into, the delicate ears that had turned a pale shade of pink.

"Who told you I wouldn't sell my share of the business?" Her gaze seemed to be directed at the distant vineyard. "It wasn't Jason, was it?"

"No," he admitted. And his chagrin was as much for the fact that it was Callie who'd recalled him to the business at hand when his mind had wanted to linger on other thoughts, as for the fact that she was right.

"Do you always rely on second-hand information?"

He wasn't going to let her make this about him. "I have no doubt about the credibility of my sources."

She studied him thoughtfully for a few seconds before speaking again. "I'm sure you trust your sister." It was no great surprise that she'd figured that much out, and he quelled the flare of admiration. "But either she's drawing inferences that are incorrect, or Jason isn't telling her the full story." She paused, thinking. "I don't think he would outright lie to either of you, he's not dishonest, but he's extraordinarily skilled at not revealing information that reflects badly on himself. It comes down to a kind of insecurity, and a need for control."

"Spare me the psychoanalysis of your ex-boyfriend." The thought of her with Jason bothered him more than it should. "Are you saying you *are* willing to sell your share of the business?"

"No." Her answer was quick.

"Then he is telling the truth?"

"No."

Nick raised an eyebrow.

She folded her arms across her chest, full breasts lifted beneath the soft cotton of her T-shirt. Had she done that deliberately? As a diversionary tactic it was incredibly effective. He trained his gaze on her narrowed eyes, could see no duplicity, only indignation.

"I don't have to explain myself to you. I suggest you talk to your new brother-in-law."

Her weary frustration wasn't going to sway him. Nick pulled his phone from his pocket. "Should I cancel my flight?" He almost wanted to. It would mean more time sparring with her. But he knew once again that that was his libido speaking.

"Put the phone away, the intimidation attempts are growing tiresome."

He hid his surprise. If circumstances were different, he could enjoy crossing swords with this woman. She was quick, insightful and definitely no pushover.

Callie uncrossed her arms and placed her palms flat on the table, making it rock and threatening her drink again. "Check your facts," she challenged. "Ivy Cottage PR is *my* business. I started it, I built it up. Jason came into it later and was a big part of the business—the front man, keeping in good with the media, the suave salesman charming the clients." Nick thought of Melody and how Jason had swept her off her feet.

Callie continued. "But I'm the creative side. I do the planning and the actual work. The agreement I had with Jason was for him to sell his share of the business to me. Only, he's changed his mind about the price we agreed on and now wants far more than his share is worth. The business is doing well, but I can't carry that kind of financial burden." The frustration was clear in her voice. "That's as much as I'm prepared to tell you. If you're still interested in hearing more of the sorry details, take it up with him."

Check your facts, she'd said. Usually he knew every nuance, every possible angle of any deal he was interested in. Today he was acting only on Melody's say-so. And although Melody was genuinely worried, she could sometimes be too quick to react. He didn't want to doubt his sister, but he wanted to believe this woman with the fire in her eyes too. Wanted to with a need that went deeper than it should. He ignored that need. He had to, at least until he knew the truth. "Rest assured I will. In the meantime, stop calling him."

"I will call my business partner whenever I deem it necessary. You have no power over me. If Jason doesn't answer my calls during the day, then I'll try him at night."

Her defiance shouldn't have surprised him. He'd do the same were their positions reversed. Nick opened his mouth to speak, but she cut him off. "Your sister may be happy for you to interfere in her life, but rest assured, Mr. Brunicadi, I won't tolerate interference in mine." She stood up and pulled a set of car keys from her pocket. "I'm going out now. I figure that's the only way I can guarantee to free myself from your company. But I hope for both our sakes you catch your flight, because I never want to lay eyes on you again."

If he challenged that assertion, if he stood and curved his hand around her neck, touched his lips to hers, how would she react? He shouldn't even want to know.

She may not want to tolerate what she called his interference, but he did what he needed to protect those he loved. He stayed seated while she stalked away, all long legs and bouncing ponytail. At the top of the steps she paused, then turned back. "How much do you have to do with Cypress Rise wines?"

"Very little. Usually. It's Melody's baby."

Relief flashed in those liquid eyes. "Thank goodness for that."

"I'm flattered." If she'd felt something for him once, he'd surely killed it. He shouldn't feel the cold sense of loss.

"You've got to admit it would be extremely uncomfortable."

He shrugged. "It could be. For as long as you're a part of Ivy Cottage, or for as long as your firm has Cypress Rise's business."

She walked back toward him with slow, deliberate footsteps, studying his face. "Is that a threat? Will you move the account because of what happened between us or because of baseless accusations?"

"We make business decisions based on sound reasoning." He didn't tell her that any decision would be made by Melody alone, and Melody wanted only the best for Cypress Rise. That was why she'd chosen Ivy Cottage PR in the first place, and she'd been more than happy with that choice. "It was merely an observation. The PR industry is notoriously fickle."

"Actually, I've found my clients to be incredibly loyal."

"Then you're very lucky."

"Or very good, Mr. Brunicadi. I believe you're aware of the award I won recently."

He almost smiled. That was the second time she'd called him Mr. Brunicadi, as though belated formality could somehow erase the intimacy of what they'd shared. "Given our past, I think you can call me Nick. And I'm well aware of how good you are."

He saw by the widening of her eyes and the heightening of her color that she'd caught the double entendre. "Leave the paper behind." She did an admirable job of speaking through clenched teeth. "Don't do the crossword. And shut the gate behind you when you go out." Chin high and back ramrod straight, she stalked off again and disappeared around the side of the house. A minute later, an engine roared into life and a silver Triumph MG, old but in good condition, sped down the driveway, kicking up a cloud of dust in its wake.

A little over a week later, Callie swung her car into the Ivy Cottage parking lot. As always, she felt a swelling of pride at the sight of her business. Everything from the gardens to the sign-written exterior was both professional and welcoming.

She'd been nineteen when she first resolved never to be dependent on someone else for her livelihood. Her PR firm was the end result of that promise to herself. Over the years the business had had its ups and downs, but she'd hung in there and weathered the storms.

The last twelve months with Jason's leaving hadn't been easy—his departure had made several clients edgy, but they were pulling through. And last week's award had already proved good for business. There had been a marked increase in calls from prospective clients. That type of acknowledgment was also reassuring for existing clients. She knew they were happy with her work, because she got results, but independent validation never hurt.

Swinging her satchel, she pushed open the front door and surveyed the reception area—the comfortable leather couches, the apricot roses in a vase on the coffee table. Shannon looked up from her computer screen, her dark hair spiky and with a hint of—was that blue?—in it. "How was your weekend?" Callie asked. Shannon's weekends were invariably more interesting than Callie's, sometimes scarily so.

"Great. But don't worry. I didn't do anything you wouldn't do." Shannon grinned, an impish smile that made her look so very young. Given that Shannon could have no idea what Callie had done at Jason's wedding, she oughtn't to be worried by that reassurance. "What about you?" Shannon asked. "Any hot dates?"

"You know I don't do hot dates." The wedding incident couldn't even be classed as a date. Were there no bounds to her shame?

"You should, and when you were late I thought maybe finally…"

Callie laughed, the sound forced to her ears. "I overslept. And not," she forestalled Shannon, "because I'd been out on a hot date. It happens sometimes."

"Yeah. But not to you."

"I'm human too."

"No." Shannon threw up her hands in mock horror, then dropped them to her desk to give herself a shove and send her chair coasting backward. "I'll get you some coffee. And I bet you didn't have breakfast, either, if you overslept."

It felt odd being mothered by someone ten years her junior. "You're right. I didn't. I'll get something from Dan the Sandwich Man when he calls in. And maybe tea rather than coffee." Coffee hadn't been sitting all that well with her the last few days. "I'll leave a couple of dollars with you and you can get me a muffin from Dan. He always seems to give you a particularly good deal."

Shannon smiled. "He likes my bad-girl looks. The nerdy ones have always been attracted to me."

The phone rang and Shannon picked it up. She held up her hand in a stop gesture as Callie was about to head into her office. "I'll check for you, sir, but her schedule is quite full today."

She hit the hold button and looked at Callie. "A man called Nick. He seems to think you'll make time to see him. Sounds like the guy who was looking for you the day of the awards dinner. Not bad-looking, either. For an old guy."

Tension seized Callie at the very mention of his name. What did he want this time? Whatever it was, she wasn't ready to see him. It was that very reluctance that made her realize she'd best get this over and done with. Besides, he'd already demonstrated he didn't take no for an answer. "I can give him ten minutes at ten o'clock, otherwise it'll have to be tomorrow." She ignored the surprised lift of Shannon's dark eyebrow and pushed through her office door and away from her scrutiny.

A few minutes later Shannon brought in a cup of tea and confirmation of her ten o'clock appointment. Her watchful silence was curious. Callie ignored it.

If only it was as easy to ignore the threat of an impending meeting with Nick Brunicadi. She was supposed to be working on a point-of-sale brochure for a farm machinery company, but her progress was almost nonexistent.

When Shannon tapped on her open office door Callie jumped, then quickly regained her composure. "Send him in," she said coolly.

"Dan?"

"Dan?" she repeated, uncomprehending at first. "Oh." She got to her feet, glad of the distraction.

Marc, her graphic designer, made an appearance in the reception area at the same time as Callie, and together they pondered what suddenly felt like a vital decision. An apricot Danish or a date scone?

Opting for one of each, Callie was standing with her hands full when the front door swung open and Nick, radiating purpose, strode in. For a second, the four of them already in reception, froze.

Shannon was the first to recover, discreetly placing her cinnamon bun out of sight on her desk. "Good morning. You must be Nick."

He nodded, then looked at Callie, making her feel guilty with the lift of one dark eyebrow and a glance at her full hands. "I can see why you could only spare ten minutes."

She refused to be cowed. Transferring the scone to the Danish hand, she held her chin high and her right hand out. Nick's gaze raked over her, taking in her dark pants and jacket. If only she'd worn higher shoes, that way she might at least be able to look him in the eye. With a smile she didn't trust for a minute, he stepped closer to enfold her hand in his. He held on for several beats too long, heat infusing what she'd intended to be a cool, professional handshake. His expression was far too complacent and far too unsettling because of it.

Callie broke the contact. "I'm surprised to see you again so soon."

"Not a pleasant surprise?" One corner of his lips tugged upward.

"Not at all," she agreed.

The wolfish smile grew. The dimple dimpled.

Damn him. He would make beautiful babies.

The thought ricocheted through her, accompanied by the knowledge that her next period was now a couple of days late. But it had been late before. She wasn't letting it mean anything.

Callie pushed the thoughts aside and strove for calm indifference. "I thought we'd said all we had to say to each other."

"We're only just beginning."

Those four words blew any hope of calmness or indifference right out of the water and froze her to the spot. Silence stretched between them.

"I can say what I need to out here if you like." Nick looked around the reception, took in the unabashedly curious faces of Shannon, Dan and Marc. "I thought, however, you'd prefer to have this conversation in private."

Callie considered her options—it didn't take long.

She gestured to her open door. "Come through to my office." The invitation was made grudgingly, but she had to get him away from Shannon.

More than once, Callie had lectured Shannon on the beauty of a committed relationship. She didn't want the girl knowing that Callie hadn't been able to live up to her own standards.

"Coffee?" Shannon asked, her gaze keen.

"That won't be necessary. I'm sure whatever Mr. Brunicadi wishes to discuss won't take long." It went against the grain to be deliberately inhospitable to a client, but Nick was the exception to the rule. She needed him gone. His mere presence caused such a complicated slew of emotions that she scarcely knew how to react—anger, defensiveness, guilt and below it all a charged sensual awareness. She couldn't help noting the strength in the clean line of his jaw, the breadth of his shoulders. She could still almost feel the clasp of his hand around hers.

With a quiet click, she shut the door behind them, enclosing them both in the suddenly too-small space of her office. Needing the physical barrier, she moved to stand behind her desk and folded her arms across her chest. "What do you want?"

He turned from his perusal of the awards and certificates hanging on her wall, his expression unreadable. It had been bad enough a week ago, when he'd been on her veranda; this was worse. Was it really as easy as it seemed for him to put thoughts of what they'd shared out of his mind? Finally, he sat in one of the leather armchairs opposite her desk, crossing his long legs at the ankles, a picture of ease.

The only thing that bolstered her confidence was

that, apart from that one error of judgment, a too hasty dance floor decision, she had done nothing wrong. Callie's hands went to her hips. "I take it you're here to apologize for your groundless accusations." She faked a nonchalance that she had yet to feel in his presence. "You must know by now that I'm not trying to keep Jason in my life. In fact, I'll be dancing on my desk for joy when I don't have to deal with him anymore." Nick raised his eyebrows, but the silence stretched, and no apology was forthcoming, so Callie continued. "If it's not that, and you're not here to tell me Jason is ready to sell, which he would have told me himself, I need to ask you to leave."

His gaze steady on her, Nick nodded his head slowly, as though in agreement, but he made no move to stand.

Callie reached for her phone. "Regardless of your threats last weekend, I *will* call security. Tell the press whatever you like. I'll deal with the consequences. Negating bad publicity is one of my strengths."

Finally, he unfolded himself from the chair and stood. But instead of heading for the door, one effortless stride had him standing right in front of her desk. He rested his fists on the top of it and leaned forward, making it suddenly hard to breathe. He was so close she could see gold flecks in his green eyes. "I have good news and bad news for you." He leaned even closer. Callie wanted to move away, but stood frozen, her heart thudding in her chest. "Do you have a preference?" he asked quietly.

"My preference is for you to leave." She reached for her phone. "Will you go, or shall I make that call?"

Unhurriedly, Nick straightened. He picked up the peace lily from her desk, shifted it to the top of her filing cabinet, nudging aside the asymmetrical award she'd won a little over a week ago to accommodate the plant.

"What are you doing?" Her hand tightened on the phone, but she watched in a kind of morbid fascination.

"Clearing your desk for you."

"Why?"

Finally he turned, riveting his attention on her. "The good news is Jason has agreed to sell his share of Ivy Cottage."

Callie let go of the phone. She should have felt a surge of elation and relief; her business would be fully back under her control, her contact with Jason would be over, but there was something about the way Nick continued to study her, like a jungle cat toying with its prey. "And the bad news is?"

He smiled. "He's sold it to me." He held out his hand, palm up. "Shall I help you onto the desk?"

Four

"No." Callie dropped into her chair and then stood again, thinking for an awful moment that she was going to be sick. She glanced at the door that would take her to the bathroom, but through sheer determination she stayed in place and the nausea subsided. The sense of shock remained. "That's not possible," she said quietly. This couldn't be happening. Not with Nick, the man who was supposed to be one night of passion and nothing more. Her guilty secret.

He said nothing as his green eyes assessed her, their calmness a counterpoint to her turmoil.

"Jason wouldn't be able to sell without my knowledge." Her voice rose and she fought to keep it under control, to keep *herself* under control. "We had an agreement. A contract." She studied the face of the man shaking the foundations of her world.

Finally, expression showed as a disapproving frown creased Nick's brow. "The agreement you had with Jason was lamentably sloppy. Though I've seen it before," he said thoughtfully. "Agreements set up between two people who trust each other, no checks and balances, no provision for a change in the relationship. Very naive. You should have kept more control."

"No." The denial sprang again from her lips. Not a denial of her naïveté, or her trusting in Jason, but another gut-level denial that this could be happening at all.

Nick didn't contradict her with words, just that steady gaze that told her he wasn't joking and that he was utterly confident of his position.

Legs weak, Callie lowered herself to her chair. The awful realization churned in her stomach. He was right, of course. Jason had been responsible for drawing up their agreements, had used a lawyer friend of his who'd given them a great price. She hadn't foreseen a time when one of them might want to sell. They had, as Nick said, trusted each other. Or she at least had trusted him. "But Jason wouldn't do that without telling me. It's my business."

"Correction, it's ours." Nick sat down again and gestured to the phone. "But please, call him for verification if you like. However, it would seem that pleasing his new brother-in-law, in whose company he now has a lucrative position, was more important than pleasing his ex-girlfriend." Even though it had gotten him what he wanted, Nick spoke the words with a hint of distaste.

Callie's heart sank. Wasn't that just like Jason, always one eye on the main chance? He was principled, but only to a point. And that point usually involved money. "You bribed him."

Nick showed no reaction. "I gave him options. The

choice was his. It didn't seem a particularly difficult one for him."

She hadn't thought Jason still had the power to hurt her, but this final betrayal proved how wrong she'd been. The years they'd shared meant that little to him. Callie looked at Nick, shaking her head in disbelief. "Why have you done this?" She could understand why Jason had sold out, but what did Nick want?

He leaned back and gave a disinterested shrug. "Control, leverage. I don't like my family being threatened."

"No one was threatening your family. Didn't you talk to Jason? Didn't he tell you that what little remained of our relationship was friendship?"

"I talked to him. And he was quite convincing. But then he would be, wouldn't he? I'm his new brother-in-law. And his boss. We come back to the fact that rightly or wrongly, Melody feels threatened."

"Wrongly." Callie thumped a fist on her desk.

The gaze that had followed her fist came back to her face. "All the same," Nick's voice was quiet, reasoned, "I thought an element of control would help ensure that things run smoothly."

"They were running smoothly."

"And long may they continue to do so."

It was probably a good thing that he'd cleared the top of her desk, because otherwise she'd surely have thrown something at him by now. "I know that you buy and sell companies all the time. But this is my business. It means everything to me. My staff are like family." She held his gaze before adding, "I can't work with you."

"I understand what you're saying. Anticipated it even, and the solution is simple."

Callie held her head in her hands, foreboding crashing down on her. He was going to force her out. She would lose everything she'd worked so hard for. She looked up, met that implacable gaze. "Will you pay me what you paid him?"

He shook his head. "That's not how it's going to work."

And she wasn't even going to get properly compensated. "You expect me to just walk away. I have responsibilities, people and their businesses depending on me."

His eyes widened slightly in surprise. "I'm not a monster, Callie. I did do some research. It didn't take long to realize you were right about being the driving force behind this business. It's clear how hard you've worked at it. I also have an inkling of what it means to you."

She let her expression speak her disbelief.

"I don't want anything to do with the day-to-day running of the business. I do expect a reasonable rate of return, as with any venture I buy into, but as long you ensure that, and have no further contact with Jason or Melody, then I'll stay out of your hair."

"Cypress Rise is a client, remember. Contact with Melody is necessary. Unless you're taking the account away?"

"I have no problems with you keeping the account, so long as someone else does the liaison."

How she'd love to throw the account back in his face. But she couldn't. It meant too much to her business. "The Jazz and Art festival is on in less than a month," she reminded him. If she left now it would throw it into chaos. The biggest loser would be its charitable recipient, the Mary Ruth Home, a shelter for runaway teenagers.

"Do what needs to be done, but have someone else liaise with the winery." He made it sound so simple.

"Is your sister really that insecure? She always struck me as confident and capable." On the surface, Melody appeared to have it all: a background of privilege, looks and a career she seemed passionate about.

Nick sat straighter, his gaze cool. "She is confident and capable. In business. In her personal life she isn't always so confident. She has her reasons. If it's in my power to protect her, then I will."

"I don't want you breathing down my neck."

His gaze dropped to her throat, then flicked back to her eyes.

He remembered. He might not want to any more than she did, but he recalled their fleeting intimacy. She wasn't sure whether that was a good thing or a bad thing.

"It's a relative term. I have, because circumstances warranted it, bought into this business—" he looked critically about her office "—with rather less information than I would usually insist on." His gaze came back to her face. "I've had to take Jason's assurances and publicly available information as fact."

"You're expecting sympathy?"

He almost smiled. Amusement flickered in his eyes, then was gone. "There are two ways of doing anything, Callie, the easy way and the hard way."

"Meaning do it your way, or you'll make it difficult, if not impossible, for me?"

"I have a half share in your business. Either one of us can make this difficult for the other. But I don't see why we should. You get the backing of a silent partner and I get—"

"Control. Leverage."

"Precisely. All I want from you at this point is information. Once I'm satisfied I know all that I should, I'll back off and leave you to it."

Would he let it be that simple? "What is it you want to know?"

"It's a little late for due diligence, but I'd like some more detail on what I've bought into. How about we start by you showing me the financial records?"

Callie stood and considered her options as she watched that impassive face, that deceptively calm gaze. She'd been on the dance floor with him, but she could see no sign of that man. *Freedom, he'd said. Hah!* Now she felt like she was in the boxing ring with him.

She could refuse, but it would serve no purpose. Reeling and tight-lipped, she strode past him to her credenza, pulled out a bound booklet and held it out to him. If she gave him this, then maybe they could both retreat to their corners and she'd have time to figure out what was happening, and more importantly, what she was going to do about it.

He took the book from her and tapped it thoughtfully. "May as well give me the last five years." He spoke casually, as though asking for nothing more than a second cup of coffee.

"We've only been going five years." Callie couldn't quite keep the exasperation from her voice.

"Even better."

Wordlessly, she turned back to the credenza and found the reports he was asking for, holding on to the thought that as soon as he was gone, she could call her lawyer and find a way out of this mess.

"So, I can work here?"

Was he baiting her? She glared at him, but could

read nothing in his green eyes. "Of course you can't. I have meetings in here."

He kept that disconcerting gaze on her. "We could enjoy working together, Callie."

She took a deep breath, but this time couldn't help rising to the bait. "We won't be working together. And we won't be enjoying anything. Take those reports and go."

"You're not going to introduce me to *our* staff?"

She couldn't conceal her horror at the prospect. "Not today."

"I'll have questions." He tapped the reports. "We should make a time for another meeting."

The phone on her desk rang with the tone for an internal call and she snatched it up. "Mr. Keane from the rafting company," came Shannon's voice.

"I'll be with him in a minute." She turned to Nick. "Now, if you wouldn't mind leaving." She pointed, stiff-armed, to the door. "Call me if you have questions."

"Perhaps you should give me your home number?"

"Like you don't already have it?"

And this time, despite how quickly he repressed it, there was no doubting the amusement that creased the corners of his eyes. She wouldn't be surprised if he'd had an entire dossier compiled. He probably knew what she ate for breakfast and the color of her underwear. Correction, he already knew that. And she only had herself to blame.

He nodded. "You'll be hearing from me." He headed toward the door.

Callie stepped out from behind her desk, took a few steps after him. "But so long as I continue to run the business well, you'll stay out of it?" She needed that as-surance. She wasn't worried about having nothing further to do with Jason or Melody; she could manage that side of things. She was, however, worried about having to confront Nick on any regular basis. Having to pretend what had happened between them hadn't, constantly feeling the pull of an attraction that was as unwanted as it was undeniable, would be torture.

He paused, turned back to her. "It's a promise."

"And I'm supposed to accept you at your word?"

"You haven't got a lot else to go on."

"There's not much reassurance in that." She shook her head. The enormity of what was happening, to her business and therefore her life, was slowly sinking in.

Something softened in his expression. "I'm as good as my word, Callie."

"Like you said, I'll have to take that."

"Believe it or not, I have a business of my own to run. A corporation that's far more important to me than this." He nodded at the financial reports in his hands, as though that was all her business boiled down to.

He was almost close enough that she could grab the lapels of his expensive suit and shake him. "You're acting like this is no big deal."

Understanding passed through his eyes. "It doesn't have to be a big deal. My stake in Ivy Cottage is an insurance policy for my sister's peace of mind. And just like with my insurances, once I know exactly what I'm getting for my money, I'm happy to pay the premiums and forget about them." He reached for the door handle, and with a nod in her direction, turned and left.

Callie stared at the door as he closed it gently behind him. If only it would be as easy for her to forget about *him*.

Five

By Sunday afternoon, through grimly determined effort, several ruined canvases and a month's worth of painting supplies, Callie had succeeded in blocking thoughts of Nick from her mind. So much so that the insistent knocking on her door startled her. Horrified, she glanced at her watch. He was early, but only by five minutes. She had no time to change, no time to mentally prepare herself. With care born of a desire to delay the inevitable, she put down her brush and wiped suddenly clammy hands on her stained shirt. Taking a deep breath, she headed resolutely for the door.

Nick had wanted to meet again, and this afternoon had been the only time that worked for both of them. Usually, she refused to let work intrude on her Sundays, but in this case it suited her well enough. She hadn't yet told Shannon and Marc that there was a new stakeholder in the business. If Nick came to Ivy Cottage again there would be no avoiding that revelation, he'd make sure of it. As it was, Shannon's pointed questions had already been hard for Callie to deflect.

As Callie opened the door, Nick, who had been looking in the direction of the neighbor's property, turned toward her. The sight of him momentarily took her breath away. His suave masculinity would be at home in an ad for European cars. His own European car, parked beyond him on the driveway, gleamed in the sunlight.

He lifted his sunglasses and his gaze found hers, his eyes green and calm. He nodded. "Callie."

"Nick." She tried to hide a reaction to his presence that was almost physical, a leaping to alert of all her senses.

This was the first time she'd seen him dressed casually. A black knit shirt stretched across his contoured chest, a heavy silver watch encircled his tanned wrist. He wore dark pants and leather shoes.

His gaze swept over her, took in her unruly hair, her oversize, paint-smeared shirt, her bare feet, before coming to rest back on her face. The contrast between them couldn't be greater. A faint smile tugged a corner of his mouth up and one eyebrow lifted. She stood back from the door, resisting the urge to respond to that smile and to explain her appearance. "Come in."

He stepped over the threshold. "So, no joy wriggling out of the agreement." It was a statement of fact.

"Trust me, it wasn't for lack of trying." She'd spent the best part of the intervening week in ultimately fruitless meetings and phone calls with her lawyer.

"I expected nothing less from you."

Surely she was mistaken in thinking the glint in his eyes might be admiration.

"But when I do something, I do it properly."

And suddenly she was remembering how thoroughly and well he had loved—no, not loved, *pleasured*—her the night of Melody's wedding.

Callie glanced at the clutch of reports in his hands. "Let's get this over with." Stepping away from his latent intensity, she led the way to the villa's cool kitchen, acutely aware of his presence behind her, of his scrutiny.

"Nice place."

"I rent it." She'd been here nearly a year, and loved the villa's spacious Old-World charm. It was far enough out of the city that visitors didn't often call. She liked that about it too.

"Who from?" The interest in his voice, in his eyes, seemed genuine, and she had to guard against it.

"A neighbor. Who, sadly, wants to sell it in six months." She glanced back, saw that Nick had stopped in front of a painting. It was one of her own, abstract, completed entirely in varying shades of blue and green.

"It reminds me of the sea."

Callie paused, then told herself it was no big deal. Art spoke to different people in different ways.

"Of the water at Cathedral Cove," he added thoughtfully as he studied it. "I visited an American colleague holidaying in that area last month."

A shiver passed through her.

"What's wrong?" he asked.

She shook her head and started walking again. "Nothing."

"Did you do it?" His voice was nonchalant.

"Yes." Given the state of her shirt, there was no point trying to hide the fact that she painted. But her art was personal, not something she liked to share. It was her version of therapy, colors expressing her moods and emotions. Six months ago she'd had a ceremonial burning of the awful, somber ones she had painted after her breakup with Jason. Today, fiery oranges and reds had dominated.

She pulled open the refrigerator. "Can I get you a drink?"

When he didn't answer she looked around the fridge door, to see him studying another of her paintings. Slowly, he turned toward her. "No, thanks."

And if she was going to be polite he could jolly well do the same. She pulled a jug of water from the fridge. "If you're going to be my business partner then we at least need to be amicable in each other's company."

"This is amicable." He dropped the reports onto the breakfast bar.

Resisting the urge to snort, she tilted her head to the side and regarded him. "All the veiled threats were amicable?"

A faint smile lifted his lips. "It's all in the interpretation. Solitude or loneliness, threat or opportunity."

Solitude or loneliness. She knew only too well where that had come from, and she didn't want him going down that track. "Please don't remind me of that night. I try never to think of it." She wasn't particularly successful, but she really did try.

He regarded her thoughtfully. "Whereas I take great pleasure in remembering it."

Callie's throat ran dry. Just looking at him, the green of his eyes, the smile that lurked there, the small V of skin revealed by the few undone buttons.... "You shouldn't. We're business partners."

"Don't you sometimes remember it? Perhaps when you're supposed to be thinking of something else entirely, you find yourself instead remembering how we—"

"No. Never." She had to cut him off, because there was something about him, something enthralling, that slipped through her self-possession, her determination. He was more relaxed today, and that made him all the more dangerous.

He met her gaze and knew she was lying.

She looked away and poured ice water into two tall glasses. "Thank you," he said with a hint of irony.

She gritted her teeth. "I need to change my shirt. You might like to wait on the veranda." She had planned on them sitting at her dining table, but she suddenly didn't want to be in a confined space with him.

He shook his head. "I'm fine here."

"And it might be construed as ill-mannered to stay in someone's kitchen when quite clearly they don't want you there."

"The veranda you say?" The small smile stretched, revealing the satisfaction he got from unsettling her.

"It's shaded and cool."

"And presumably I should take my drink?"

"Yes."

Still smiling, he gathered up the reports and strolled back the way they'd come. Stalling for time, Callie washed her hands and changed her shirt, vacillating over her decision. The clothes and makeup she wore during the week were her armor, and if ever she'd needed armor it was now. But on the other hand, she didn't want Nick reading insecurity or a desire to impress him into her choice. In the end she opted for a T-shirt and her favorite jeans.

All the while her thoughts were on Nick, outside, waiting. And his smile. Did he know how it weakened her?

She shook her head. This was a simple business meeting; nothing she couldn't handle. It was on her territory, it was about her business, and she would be able to answer any questions he had. Though it would help if she had some idea what those questions might be.

And it would help even more if she didn't still have that other worry—the one about her now undeniably late period—hanging over her head. She'd gone so far as to buy a pregnancy test kit. It sat unopened in her bathroom cabinet. But as long as it remained unopened she could believe—hope—she was safe.

Nick stood on the veranda and surveyed the rolling hills that surrounded Callie's place, so much greener than those back in Australia. He saw again the neighboring vineyard, the grass around the vines still too long. The only sound was the rustling of leaves in a nearby stand of poplar trees. Some of the tension he hadn't realized he was carrying seeped from his shoulders. He could see why she liked it here.

At the sound of the door opening he turned. Clutching her glass of water as tightly as she had her champagne the night of the wedding, Callie stepped onto the veranda. Her dark curls were loose about her face, jeans, faded with washing, molded to the flare of her hips, a white T-shirt skimmed oh so gently over her curves, its neckline at the base of her throat.

He'd never before met anyone who could make demure look so utterly sexy.

Business. This was about business, he reminded himself forcefully. He was good at compartmentalizing.

Usually.

She met his gaze calmly, but her throat betrayed her with small, nervous swallows. Nick smiled. Complacent. If the business at hand happened to give him a little advantage over Calypso Jamieson, helped her see that he wasn't someone to be trifled with, then so much the better.

Yet so much about her resonated with him. The work she'd done on the Cypress Rise account had captured the essence of the winery. What he had been able to glean about the way she ran her business struck a chord of familiarity, the paintings that hung in her home spoke to him, the depths in her chocolate-colored eyes haunted him. Even that smudge of red she'd missed beneath her jaw affected him, made him want to reach out and touch it. Touch her. As though it was his right.

He couldn't shake the feeling that stirred whenever he saw her, a feeling of connection.

Acting on that feeling had caused this mess in the first place.

He could make her regret walking out on him, but knew that the distance she wanted to keep between them was for the best. She wasn't the type of woman he got involved with. Contrary to what he'd thought the night of the wedding, she was long-term, the sort who made deep and permanent connections. Many of her clients had been with her from day one. And she was a nester. It was obvious in the way she'd used personal touches to turn this rented villa into more of a home than the designer apartment he'd owned for six years.

Nick had believed both Jason's and Callie's assurances that there was nothing left between them. But he didn't quite trust his own need to believe. That was one of the reasons he'd bought the share of her business. There was logic in having that insurance policy, even though the part of him that insisted on honesty told him there was more than just that to his decision.

For the moment though, things were back under his control. And he liked to have control—of the beginnings, the middles and the ends.

Callie set her water down carefully, then frowning, looked beneath the table to see the folded paper he had wedged beneath one of the legs to minimize the wobble. She glanced quickly toward him. "It's not perfect and it's only temporary," he said.

"I've been meaning to fix that," she said, then took a deep breath. "Thank you." He suppressed the urge to smile at how much the words seemed to cost her. They would get this meeting over and done with and that would be it. It needed to be, because he liked just being with her far too much.

He pulled out a chair for her, caught a faint trace of her perfume as she passed close by him to sit.

"So what are these questions?" She looked at the reports that lay between them, touched a slender finger, stained a faded red, to the brightly colored markers protruding from beneath the covers.

"How about you give me a little background on the business to start with. The personal side."

"It's not all there in the numbers?"

"The numbers tell a story. But I'd like to know what's behind them. How did you start up? How long have Shannon and Marc been with you? What's your style of doing business?"

"You don't want much, do you?" Gentle sarcasm laced her words.

He ignored it as he ignored the other wants that were always present when she was near.

"How much time have you got?"

Nick leaned back in his chair and stretched his legs out. "As long as it takes."

She sighed, her gaze flicked to him and then away, and she started telling him about the business, her story hesitant and factual at first. But as he asked questions she seemed to forget who she was talking to. He listened to her mistakes and her successes with equal attention. He could understand how tough it had been in the early days and admired the way she had hung in there.

He teased out the details and stories of Ivy Cottage's history. His opinion should only matter because, the more confidence he had in her, the easier it would be to leave her alone. She was careful also to give credit to Jason. He didn't mind the sense that it was begrudgingly given. Her ex-partner had done her no favors. Nick liked his new brother-in-law a little less for that fact.

Somewhere in the telling of her story, her stance shifted from defensive to conspiratorial.

Nick forgot the passage of time. Could just be with her, listening to her, laughing with her. Watching her.

He didn't realize how long they had sat talking till she looked up, and he followed her glance, to see the orange glow of sunset coloring the horizon. She touched her fingers to her lips in surprise. "I'm sorry. I didn't mean to talk for so long, and we haven't even got to the reports."

He shook his head, leaned forward in his seat. "Don't worry about the time on my account." He captured her wide brown gaze with his own. "I'm only going back to my hotel room. But what about you? You have your painting to do."

Her lips parted, but it wasn't until she broke the contact of their gaze that words came out. "It hardly matters now. I've lost the light."

He knew he disconcerted her, that beneath her efficient facade shimmered an awareness she wanted to deny. He wasn't going to let her, not completely. But he needed to retain the upper hand, and talk of darkness and hotel rooms could too easily lead his thoughts down dangerous paths. Time to redirect them. "Have you always painted?"

"For as long as I can remember. I even started a fine arts degree."

There was something wistful in her tone. "Started?"

She frowned. "I changed to commerce." And suddenly her tone was as businesslike as her degree.

"Why?"

"Because there's a livelihood in it." Again the serious tone. Her hands had gone to her hips.

"Who are you quoting?"

Her eyes widened.

"Weren't you quoting someone just then?"

She tipped her head to one side and studied him. A rueful smile touched her lips as she nodded once. "My mother's partner at the time."

"You changed your degree to please someone else?"

She shrugged. "Not exactly. But he'd been made redundant, and he helped me see that I needed something solid to rely on, something I had control over. It made sense to study commerce."

"Not if it wasn't what you really wanted to do." He suddenly laughed, surprising himself as much as her.

"What's so funny?"

"That advice coming from me. I chose the university I attended because of someone else."

"What do you mean?"

He looked out over the hills. "My girlfriend at the time wanted to study at Adelaide, so I went there too. To be with her." This was a definite foray into the personal, a shifting of the ground.

"If you were choosing universities together, you must have been practically childhood sweethearts."

"Something like that."

"What happened to her?" Callie's tone was teasing.

"She left me for an affair with her English professor." It was the last, the only time, he'd been the one to be left.

"Bad trade."

Nick looked sharply at her, expecting to discern sarcasm. But her gaze was serious. He allowed himself a smile. "I like to think so." But he regretted the confidence he'd shared. Why Callie? Why had he told this woman what he never talked about? The past was past, and certainly had no place here. His uncharacteristic loss of focus could only have been caused by the woman opposite him, by the way her softly parted lips made him long to cover them with his own.

He pulled the top report off the small stack. "This shouldn't take long. Clarify a couple of anomalies I've found, and then you needn't see me again. We can both get on with what we do best." He'd found enough in his reading of the reports, and from talking to her and others in the industry, to know the business was in capable hands.

"That's a promise?"

She wanted to end the contact too. The fleeting closeness of this afternoon had been an illusion. "You won't even have to see me in person—phone and e-mail should be all we need." Impersonal. Freedom for both of them.

Callie studied him. It was strange to think of him

hurting. He seemed so strong, so impervious. The warmth she'd felt only minutes earlier in his presence had cooled. But over the last couple of hours, she had come to realize that he didn't have to be an adversary, could in fact be an ally. Through talking they'd reached a tenuous understanding. She could trust him and his word. She would be able to run her business how she wanted, and she wouldn't have Nick's constant presence to remind her of that one mistake.

That one night of magic.

He turned back the cover on the first report and she leaned forward, resting her elbows on the table so that she could read the small print better. The table wobbled slightly. She straightened in remembered reflex, and her arm collided with her glass, sending it flying. It crashed onto the wooden boards, shattering on impact.

Callie dropped to the floor, began picking up the larger pieces. Nick crouched opposite her. "Leave it," she instructed him. "I'll fix it."

He ignored her and picked up another shard.

They reached for the same piece at the same time and his fingers brushed hers. She glanced up to see if he, too, had felt that jolt of heat. His gaze was steady on her. Pulse pounding, Callie scooted back. Her heel caught on an uneven board and she started to fall. Her hands flew out to break her backward tumble and glass sliced into her palm.

Sitting on the wooden boards, she cradled her hand in her lap to examine it. The cut was clean, but long and deep.

Nick stepped closer. "What have you done?"

"Nothing." She let him help her to her feet. "I just need a Band-Aid." Nursing her hand and her throbbing wrist, she headed inside, dripping blood. Her T-shirt was already a mess, so, as best she could, she wadded up the fabric and held it against the cut to stanch the flow. In the bathroom, she pulled open the door of the cabinet. Grabbing a tissue, she swabbed away the blood, then found the box of Band-Aids and awkwardly extracted one and stripped the covering paper from it.

"Are you okay?" The deep voice, softened with concern, sounded close behind her.

The Band-Aid folded in on itself, sticking irretrievably. She threw it into the trash and reached for another one. "It's nothing serious."

"Do you need a hand?"

"No. Not even a finger." She pressed a tissue to the cut that still oozed blood.

Ignoring her feeble joke, Nick stepped closer, crowding her in the small bathroom. That proximity, that faint scent, overrode the pain and did straightaway what she'd earlier denied—sent her thoughts back to their first encounter, and the thrumming sensuality of it. He reached for her hand again, and this time she let him see the cut. She was beginning to think she might need more than a Band-Aid. "I've kind of hurt my wrist too."

Gently, he wiped the blood away, then, still cradling her hand in his, he looked up and met her gaze. "I'm taking you to the emergency room."

The threat of his suggestion quashed her awareness of his proximity, of the gentleness of his touch, the caring in his eyes. "I don't like doctors. Or needles."

His grip on her hand tightened. Green eyes met and held hers. "Deal with it." The sympathy stayed in his gaze. "Where's your first-aid kit? We'll do what we can here. But then you *are* going to see a doctor."

She looked at the cut again. Maybe he was right. Reluctantly, she nodded at the bathroom cabinet. "The cupboard beneath the sink. Red box. White cross on it."

Nick's half smile softened his features. He crouched down and reached into the cabinet. For a second his movements stilled, and sudden fear clenched in her chest. He stood with the first-aid kit in his hands. She couldn't see his face as he bent over her hand and deftly applied a couple of Steri-strips.

The twenty-minute trip, with her wrist iced and her hand bandaged, was made in silence. Callie knew what was in her bathroom cabinet beside the first-aid kit, could too easily picture the pristine box. She'd spent long enough staring at it over the past few days. She just didn't know whether Nick had seen it, whether he had time to read what it was.

And she wasn't about to ask him.

The A&E clinic was mercifully quiet. She filled in a form on a clipboard, and after waiting a short while a nurse approached. "If you'd like to come with me," she said, sounding far too cheery. Callie wanted to turn and run. She glanced at the door, then at Nick.

"Do you want me to come with you?" There was a tightness in his expression and a frown marred his brow. But still, he seemed the lesser of two evils. She nodded and they followed together as the nurse, her right shoe squeaking quietly with each step, led them to a room with a white-sheeted bed, a desk and a couple of chairs. The smell of disinfectant permeated the air. Callie felt the nausea rising.

"Take a seat. The doctor will be with you in a moment." The squeaks faded away down the corridor.

"How much don't you like doctors or needles?"

She didn't look at him. "It's nothing I can't handle."

Before he could question her further, the doctor appeared. He scanned the form on the clipboard, then turned to Callie. "Let's take a look at you. Why don't you sit up on the bed?"

She eased herself onto the bed, legs dangling vulnerably over the edge. The doctor carefully examined her hand and then her wrist.

"You'll need stitches, and you've sprained your wrist, but it's nothing serious," he said cheerfully, apparently having been to classes with the nurse.

Didn't they know there was nothing remotely cheery about being here, about the prospect of stitches? Callie hesitated. She looked up and saw the gaze of both the doctor and Nick on her. "Perhaps it'll be best if you lie down," the doctor suggested, a sudden wariness creeping into his expression.

Did that mean she'd gone as white as she felt? Callie was happy to oblige. She lay back on the bed and screwed her eyes shut.

"And sir," the young doctor said, "you might like to hold her other hand."

Callie opened her eyes to see both of them still watching her. She gave her head a small and apparently unconvincing shake. In two steps, Nick was at her side and took hold of her good hand. She didn't want to need anyone, and especially not him. As she was about to pull her hand from his clasp she looked across at the doctor, saw the syringe he held and felt as though she was falling. She turned her head, and her eyes found Nick's, saw strength and comfort offered in the depthless green. He was here with her for now, and this would be all right. He told her so without speaking. She closed her eyes and tightened her fingers around his hand. His thumb stroked gently across the back of her hand, warm and sure. A calmness stole through her.

That calmness had fled by the time Nick stopped his car in front of her house. "Thanks for helping me out." It was over, and now she needed to get rid of him. "You don't need to come in, I'm fine now."

He turned off the lights and cut the engine.

The silence pressed down on her. "I know I was a sissy back there, but honestly, I'm fine." Using only her left hand, she unbuckled her seat belt and opened her door. "Thanks again."

Nick opened his door and got out as she did. He looked at her across the roof of the car, his face illuminated by the sensor lighting that had come on. He did not look happy. "We haven't finished talking."

She remembered the financial reports still stacked on her outdoor table, hoped against hope that it was those reports he was referring to. Not the box in her bathroom cabinet. "The reports can wait. It's late, you must be tired. I am." She faked a yawn.

"I don't want to talk about the reports," he said quietly. He shut his car door and climbed the steps to the veranda, then stood waiting at her front door.

Callie took slow, dread-filled steps toward him. He made no move to help her as she fumbled with her key, finally slipping it into the lock and pushing the door open.

"Can I make you a drink? Tea, coffee, something stronger?"

He shook his head, lips pressed ominously together. But at least he didn't mention the box.

She didn't want a drink, either, but playing for time,

Callie filled the kettle, set it to boil. Even in the distorted reflection of the kettle's curving stainless steel she could see that he watched her. Avoiding facing him, she pulled a mug from an overhead cupboard, dropped a tea bag into it. Nick sat on a bar stool on the far side of the breakfast bar. She turned back and watched the kettle. The only sound in the room was the low whisper of the water heating and the occasional quiet drum of his fingertips on the countertop. The feeling of vertigo that had assailed her at the clinic threatened to return. Her heart thundered in her chest.

A chair leg scraped across the floor, footsteps sounded down her hallway. Perhaps he just needed to use her bathroom. Callie poured boiling water into her cup, prodded the teabag with a spoon. As the footsteps returned she dropped the sodden bag into the bin and added a dash of milk to her drink.

Finally, she could delay it no longer. Cup in her good hand, she faced the breakfast bar. Nick was seated again, watching her. On the counter in front of him sat a rectangular blue-and-white box. She dragged her gaze from the box to the man. The Nick who'd held her hand at the clinic was gone. This one's icy glare chilled her to the marrow.

"When did you buy this?"

Callie opened her mouth to answer, but no words came out. She'd only bought it a few days ago, when she could no longer ignore the lateness of her period. She quailed under his scrutiny. Could she lie, tell him that the box wasn't hers or that she'd bought it a year ago, but then never had to use it?

Tension radiated from him. "What aren't you telling me?" The question was harsh, more like an accusation.

She looked at the box. Guilt and fear rose within her. "This wasn't supposed to happen."

"What wasn't supposed to happen? Are you pregnant?"

"I don't know," she said quietly, not meeting his gaze. "That's why I bought that." She nodded at the innocuous-looking box, a cardboard grenade with the potential to explode throughout her life.

"You told me you'd had your period."

"I did." Finally she looked up. Confusion and distrust were etched on his face.

"So, how is it we're now looking at this?"

"It was a little late and very light. And I've since learned that can sometimes happen when you're pregnant, but I was hoping it wasn't the case, that it was light because of stress. But now the second period is late."

"How late?" The bluish outline of a vein pulsed in his temple.

"Two weeks."

"Why haven't you told me?"

"Because I don't know yet. Because you were celebrating your freedom. Because you don't need the worry."

"And you do?"

"I don't have a choice. And I don't have your obvious fear of commitment."

He shook his head, his expression scathing. "You don't know anything about me."

"I know enough."

He wasn't to be sidetracked. "Were you going to tell me?"

"Yes. If it turned out that I was pregnant, I would have told you."

He gave an almost imperceptible shake of his head. As though he doubted even that. His doubt cut her more than she'd thought it would. Maybe because it was at least partially deserved, or had she started liking him again, liking that respect and recognition she'd discerned in his gaze?

She had to be stronger, more insular. "It doesn't really matter now whether you believe me or not. This whole argument could be pointless. I may not even be pregnant. This is exactly what I was hoping to avoid."

"When are you planning on taking the test?"

"I thought I'd wait a few more days. Maybe a week." Keep waiting and keep hoping. As if hope alone would make her period come.

He studied her for long seconds. "Take it now."

She looked at him horrified, took a step back. "I can't."

Nick's chair scraped across the floor as he stood and strode into the kitchen. "Why not?"

Callie backed up against the counter. "I'm not ready."

"What do you have to do to be ready?"

"Nothing. I meant that I'm not ready to be a mother. To deal with that news."

He took a step closer. "And you think I'm ready to be a father?"

She looked up at him. "But you wouldn't have to—"

"Wouldn't have to what?" The sudden edge to his voice sent a chill along her spine.

"To deal with anything for a good few months yet. Everything would change for me from the moment I found out. *If* I was pregnant."

"Let's find out then."

"But—"

"You're not ready?"

Callie, usually eloquent, fell silent.

"I'll tell you what. You take the test. I'll look at the

results, and I won't tell you what they are. That way you won't have to deal with anything. When you are ready to know, you'll only need to ask."

"You know I'm not going to do that."

"That's just it, Callie. I don't know anything of the sort. I don't know you. I mean, here I am assuming that if you're pregnant then I'm the father. Is that a valid assumption? Has there been someone else before or since me?"

Her temper rose. "How dare you? If you want to deny paternity go right ahead. I won't fight you."

"But I *will* fight you if you try to deny me what is mine."

"A child is not a possession."

"I didn't suggest that. I'm talking about a child's right to a relationship with both its parents. And a parent's right to a relationship with that child. And you still haven't answered my question."

"What's the point? You clearly have trouble believing anything I say."

"Tell me, Callie. This is no time for playing games."

She met and held his gaze. "You're the only man I've slept with since I broke up with Jason. In fact, you're the only man other than Jason I've *ever* slept with. If I'm pregnant, then you are the father."

The accusation in his eyes eased. "Thank you." He said it so quietly she almost didn't hear the words. He dropped his gaze and turned the box over in his hands. In the stretching silence she heard the quiet crackle of the cellophane wrapper. Finally he spoke. "You need to take this test." He looked up. Held her gaze.

Callie swallowed. "I passed every test I ever took in school. I think this one's going to be a positive result, as well."

"You've had other symptoms?" His anger had been replaced by a kind of resignation.

"No. At least no morning sickness or weird cravings, and I don't even think my breasts have changed size." They both looked at her chest, then looked up again. "Although I have gone off coffee, and I'm sleeping more than usual."

"You're procrastinating."

She nodded. "Wouldn't you?"

"No. I want to know, so that we can deal with whatever we need to deal with. I like to face my... I like to face things head-on."

He'd been going to say "problems," she knew it. But he wouldn't be so very wrong, a pregnancy would definitely create problems. In business she told herself that problems also always presented opportunities, and if the big "if" was true, she knew in time she'd see the opportunities, that there would be a definite plus side to all this.

Nick picked up her good hand and surprisingly gently pressed the angular package into it. For a few seconds his hands, large and warm, cradled hers as she held the box. Then he released her and stepped back. "Take the test."

Six

It felt like a lifetime later when Callie stepped onto the veranda where Nick waited. The night air, warm but cooling rapidly, closed around her. A half moon hung low in the sky, only a handful of stars able to compete with its glow. She was reminded forcefully of that other night not so very long ago when it had been just the two of them on a darkened balcony.

New beginnings, new lives. They'd certainly achieved that, though not in the way either of them had imagined.

Nick stood with his back to her, staring out into the night. At first glance his stance, as he leaned against the railing, appeared relaxed. A closer look revealed tension in the muscles of his shoulders. She waited for him to turn. The beat of her heart was a slow, heavy thump.

He remained immobile.

Numb, she walked to stand beside him, followed his

gaze into the blue-black night. The song of nearby cicadas filled the air. "When I was little," she said, "I used to lie in bed at night listening to the cicadas, pretending I was Pocahontas. I thought if I listened hard enough I would hear secrets they were trying to tell me."

He turned at last and studied her. "You're pregnant."

She nodded. That blue line still seemed imprinted on her retina.

"Could it be wrong?"

She shook her head. "Not three times." She turned away as tears suddenly welled. Weren't children supposed to be a joy? All she felt was overwhelmed and more than a little frightened. She didn't know how to do this alone, to be a mother, to raise a child. Especially when her relationship with its father was so fragile.

She glanced over her shoulder at Nick, saw him still studying her. She could read nothing in his gaze, no anger, none of the fear and uncertainty she felt. She wanted to say something, but no words came. For the second time he took her hand in his, interlacing their fingers. His touch again gentle, warmth seeped into her, a physical manifestation of that unseen connection they now shared. Slowly he led her to the cane couch on the veranda. They sat down wordlessly, shoulders touching, and looked out into the night.

Drifting clouds had obscured the moon when he finally spoke. "I want what's best for our baby." His voice revealed no emotion, gave no clue as to what he thought or felt for himself.

"So do I. But I'm frightened that I don't know what that is or how to give it." In an instant her life had been turned upside down, and being pregnant felt so…huge, that it put everything she'd done before into a new perspective.

It was a long time before Nick responded. "Do you want me to take the child?"

Callie shot up from the couch and whirled to face him. "Of course not."

"I don't expect to be that bad a parent. And I can get help. A nanny?" He was still too calm.

"How can you think for one minute—"

"I was just asking." The facade cracked and frustration seeped out. "I need to know how things stand, what you want."

"I want this baby." Callie held her hands protectively over her abdomen.

In one fluid motion he was standing too. "The one mere minutes ago you didn't even want to know existed?"

"Yes, that one. Because now I do know it exists and the only thing at all I'm certain about is that I want it."

He held her gaze. "At least we're clear on that."

She turned and leaned on the veranda railing, gripped its rough solidity. Thoughts whirled in her head. "We've only known for a few minutes. It's too early to have it all sorted out. There's too much to take in, to think about." She was pregnant. There was a life growing inside her, separate from her and yet a part of her. She could barely even wrap her head around that concept.

Nick came to stand beside her, his presence solid and imposing. She'd seen the way he protected his family. No matter what her relationship with this man, she didn't doubt that their child would at least always have that fierce protection. But how would it affect her? Would he see her as an obstacle to be outmaneuvered, as he had with her business?

"So, you're willing to work things out with me on this?"

Was she being paranoid, or was that a veiled threat?

Would he be calling his lawyers first thing in the morning? "Of course I am." His offer to have the child had spooked her. Perhaps she should be the one to call her lawyer in the morning. He already had proved he was capable of taking drastic precautionary measures.

"There's no of course about it." She heard a shadow of her own uncertainty in his voice. "We don't know each other well."

"And yet here we are, partners in a business and about to have a baby."

He said nothing.

Callie filled the gaping silence. "I don't know what you expect from me, what rights you want or think you have."

"This isn't a promising start," he growled. "Do we need to talk about custody and visitation, about financial arrangements?"

"Don't, Nick." She turned to face him. "It's too soon. Can't you just…"

"Just what?"

A moth fluttered past the porch light and then out into the night. "Just leave. I need time to think." It was either ask him to leave or ask him to hold her, but she couldn't let herself need him.

He studied her. "How much time?"

She shook her head. "I don't know."

"All right," he agreed slowly. "I'll see you tomorrow then."

"Tomorrow?" What was he thinking? "No. This isn't *sleep on it and I'll have it all figured out by morning* type of news."

"I want to get this sorted out."

"So do I. But tomorrow's not enough time. Not nearly enough."

"What's more important than this?" He gestured to her stomach.

"Nothing." She fought for calm. Why wouldn't he understand? "I need time, and that's the one thing we at least have a little bit of. We don't have to have anything sorted out by tomorrow, or even the next day. It can wait. Give me…a week." She watched that impassive face. "Please?"

The frown creasing his brow advertised his reluctance to give her even that much time. He was the sort who tackled life head-on, who, if he had a problem, worked at it till he found the solution. But his way wasn't right for her. "I still have work to attend to. And unlike you, I don't have an endless stream of minions I can delegate to." Right now work was the least of her concerns, but perhaps Nick would find that excuse easier to accept.

"Will you be able to make time to go to the doctor next week? Can you fit that into your hectic schedule?"

She ignored the undertone of scorn. "I'll go to the doctor."

"I'll come with you."

"To make sure I go, or to offer support?" She thought she knew which.

A rueful smile touched his lips. "Perhaps both." The smile vanished. "I fly to San Francisco tomorrow morning for a series of meetings. If I reschedule some things I can be back by next week. Make the appointment for then."

He glanced at her stomach. Callie looked down, hadn't realized that, as they'd been speaking, she'd placed her hand over her abdomen.

When she looked up again Nick's gaze hadn't shifted, and he was reaching slowly toward her. He touched her hand with his fingertips.

He looked up and for a moment their gazes met. Did she see an echo of her own awe and wonder in his eyes? Beneath their hands lay new life.

Nick's hand dropped back to his side. "Is there anything you want me to do?"

"Like what?"

"I don't know." The words, the lack of certainty they revealed, seemed to pain him.

Callie felt a strange stirring of sympathy. She resisted the urge to step closer, to take hold of his hand once again. To give or take comfort? She wasn't sure which. So instead she stepped back, wrapped her arms about herself. "There's nothing you can do now," she spoke softly. "Except give me some space. Please."

He nodded slowly and then turned and strode away, his footsteps echoing in the night. She heard his car purr into life and watched as red taillights disappeared down her driveway.

Callie sat in her car, staring at the red brick building in front of her. She should go in. Just get out of the car, walk up the three gray concrete steps to the front door and go in. She only wished she didn't feel quite so alone, but there were no friends she wanted to share the knowledge of her situation with yet. Nor was she ready to tell her mother. She wasn't even entirely sure where her mother was right now. Her last postcard from her had been of Inca ruins in Peru.

Slowly, she unbuckled her seat belt. As she touched her fingers to the door handle her phone rang and she snatched it up gratefully. "Hello." Her greeting was quick and eager. Perhaps they needed her at work and she'd have to go.

There was a pause. "How are you?" The question earnest, seeking an honest response. The voice deep and warm. "Did you sleep last night?"

Implying that he hadn't?

She hadn't thought she wanted to hear from Nick again, and certainly not so soon. But apparently she was wrong. Her spinelessness was great enough to make his call welcome. "Better than I expected. At least the uncertainty is gone now." No more lying in bed wondering whether or not she was pregnant. Just lying in bed wondering what happens next.

"Where are you?"

The one question she hadn't wanted him to ask. Callie took a deep breath. "Outside my doctor's office. Working up the courage to go in." She glanced at the wooden front door and then at her watch.

She grimaced as she counted the seconds of the pause. Finally he spoke. "You were going to wait till I came back."

She hadn't actually agreed to that, but now probably wasn't the time to argue her point. "I'm taking a leaf out of your book. Although I'm not so sure that I like it. But now at least you won't have to cut short your trip." She glanced again at the suddenly ominous building and remembered the other proactive call she'd made. The one setting up an appointment with her lawyer. Nick sounded conciliatory now, caring even, but she'd learned her lesson—and she was going to protect herself and get good legal advice.

"I'm in the country still. Give me the doctor's address." In the background she heard a flight departure announcement.

"You're at the airport?"

"Yes, but I'll change my flight."

The offer seemed to give her strength. "Don't, but thanks," she said quietly. "It'll be okay. I'll be okay. I just have to get to the front door. And I should really do it now. My appointment's in a few minutes."

"Okay."

But neither of them hung up.

"Thanks for calling."

"Get out of the car, Callie." This time she definitely heard a smile in his voice and felt an answering tug at her lips.

"I am," she said as she opened her door and got out. "My doctor's lovely." She walked across the car park. "A gentle, older woman. She's known me for years."

"How long?" He encouraged her to talk.

"She delivered me, so she knows what she's doing." Feeling like he was at her side, Callie climbed the steps and pushed open the door. "I'll call you afterward, if there's anything I think you'd want to know."

"Call me anyway."

She called, Nick thought, as he slipped into the auditorium and stood in the shadows at the back of the crowded room. He'd give her that much. But her call had come while he'd been on the plane. She'd left a message, her voice soft and awestruck, assuring him that everything had gone well.

Soon after that she'd left a second message, professional, though vaguely defensive and full of excuses, as she listed far too many reasons why they should delay meeting again for another two weeks. He wasn't having it, so he'd flown back to Sydney where she was presenting at this conference.

And so here he was, watching as she stood in the center of the stage, exuding passion and expertise. A microphone the size of a pinot noir grape was attached to the lapel of her tailored jacket. Her dark hair was pulled sleekly back from her face. Her fitting skirt skimmed her knees. Ostensibly, there was nothing provocative about her. A pair of ankles and a shapely calf should not make his thoughts go where they were heading. Back into the land of fantasy. But he knew how soft her skin was, knew the throaty sound of her laugh. And he wanted her. The reaction was instinctive. The logical side of him could and would deny it, but it was there.

He could scarcely reconcile this polished professional with the woman with paint smears on her face, or the woman standing frightened and uncertain in the moonlight. He had ached to wrap his arms around her then, too, and just hold her, but he couldn't trust himself, he was too willing to overlook logic and reason where she was concerned.

It was almost ironic. He was usually the one who stopped people from getting too close. He knew the hurt that led to. And now Callie was trying to keep him at arm's length. She had given him no idea of whether she would want too much or not enough.

From the front of the room she glanced his way and paused a beat, but he was confident she couldn't see him. She stood in the full glare of the lights, while he was in shadow.

He hadn't missed her assertion the other night, that aside from Jason, her then partner, he was the only other man she'd slept with. It didn't seem possible. A woman this vibrant, this attractive? But the implications of that fact ran deep. She took her relationships seriously.

He frowned as he noticed the bandage on her hand, realized also that she was wielding her pointer with her left hand with a hint of slowness. Her right hand passed in front of her abdomen, still flat.

She was carrying his baby.

Regardless of what she did or didn't want, he *would* be a part—an integral part—of his child's life.

As the door to her hotel room swung shut behind her, Callie slipped out of her shoes and wriggled her toes on the carpet. She shrugged out of her jacket and tossed it onto the first of the two beds. As she was peeling off the panty hose from beneath her skirt, the phone on her bedside table rang. Still pulling the last leg of the hose off, she hopped over to the phone and dropped onto the bed as she picked up the handset. "Callie speaking."

"You made it to your room at last."

She knew that deep voice too well. "Nick?" Her pulse quickened, as it always did around him.

"You were expecting someone else?"

She stood as though that could give her the strength she needed to deal with this man. "I wasn't expecting anyone." She'd known she'd hear from him again sooner or later—she'd valiantly hoped for later.

"Even though we agreed we'd talk this week?" His voice sounded almost pleasant. Callie didn't trust it for a moment. He'd be annoyed that she'd put him off, knew that his gentleness when she'd spoken to him outside the doctor's had been a passing illusion. Not something she could, or would, want to rely on.

"I called and left you a message explaining."

"It was a cop-out, Callie. We both know that."

"It wasn't a cop-out. I didn't have my personal organizer when we agreed on this week, and you'll appreciate my thoughts were in turmoil that evening. I have it with me now—give me a second and I'll get it from my briefcase." She dropped the phone on the bed and retrieved her organizer, then switched it on as she was picking up the phone again. "I've got it in front of me, and next week is looking more flexible. Name your day."

"I don't want to leave it till next week to talk to you."

She knew better than to think that meant he wanted to see her for her own sake. "I can't see you any sooner than that. I'm tied up at a conference this week and I won't be back in the office till next week."

"You didn't mention in the message you left where the conference was."

She hesitated. The omission had been deliberate. And given that she was now on the phone to him, he obviously knew where she was. "Sydney," she said on a sigh. Sydney, where the head office of Brunicadi Investments was located.

"Then I think we should meet sooner than next week."

"Nick, I don't—" A knock sounded on her door. "Hang on a second, someone's here."

"I'll talk to you soon then." The dial tone sounded in her ear.

As she crossed to the door Callie knew he'd gone too easily. *Duh.* The unexpected knock suddenly made depressing sense. She looked through the peephole, saw him waiting in the corridor. And even through the distortion of the glass she saw that mix of careless elegance and intensity that was Nick's alone. His dark jacket hung open, revealing the white shirt beneath. She opened the door and for a second they looked at each other. Again, Callie felt the awareness that invariably rolled through her like a deep tremor whenever she saw him. Green eyes searched her face. Then, breaking that contact, he strolled in.

"I have a sponsor's dinner to go to shortly." She spoke to the back of his dark head and broad shoulders.

Nick surveyed the room. Too late, she remembered the clothes scattered around and the panty hose discarded on the floor by the phone. She also remembered that one other time she'd been in a hotel room with him. Clothes discarded then with even less thought. Her face heating, she strode past him, picked up the scattered items and dropped them into her suitcase, pushing down the lid that stood open.

"If there's such a rush, why weren't you up here earlier?" He turned and suddenly his river-green gaze held hers—dark, unreadable.

Her heart quickened, and again memories surged of that other hotel room, the penthouse suite. A gaze darkened with desire then. Callie spoke slowly, tried to make her voice sound even. "I was in the salon trying to get a hair appointment." The parameters had been set— they were business partners and accidental parents to be, nothing more. She reached behind her head and removed the clasp that held her hair in place. Unruly curls cascaded around her face. "But there's a celebrity auction for breast cancer here tonight, and they can't fit me in. And neither can any of the other nearby salons." She ran her fingers through her hair. "It needs a wash and I can't do it because I can't get this stupid hand wet." She lifted her right arm. "For which, rightly or wrongly, I hold you in part responsible."

"Why is it still like that? The stitches should have been out by now." The concern in his voice surprised her.

"It got infected." She shrugged. "It should be okay in a few more days."

His gaze shifted from her hand back to her face. "I saw your presentation this afternoon."

"That was you standing at the back of the room?"

He nodded.

She'd had a feeling that he was there, had looked for him in the audience once it was over, then decided she'd been imagining things.

Idly, he picked up her organizer from the bedside table, flipped it over to look at the back, and then replaced it before Callie could protest. He turned the full force of his attention on her. "We need to talk about your pregnancy, about our child. About what we're going to do."

Our child.

Hearing the words out loud made it so very real. She was pregnant by her client's brother, her ex-boyfriend's brother-in-law and her new business partner. She couldn't have made this any messier if she'd tried.

Callie crossed to the small sink and poured herself a glass of water. She spoke to the tap. "I've hardly been able to think about anything else. Anytime I have a moment to myself, that's where my thoughts go. But once there, they circle around and around." The words tumbled from her. "I haven't got any answers. I don't know how to make this work. How you and I can be the parents we each want to be? How to run a business and be a mother at the same time?" It felt so good to let the words and her confusion out. No one else knew she was pregnant. She wasn't ready to share the news, but that also meant she had no one to talk to. She turned to find Nick standing inches in front of her, looking down at her, his brow furrowed.

Any further words died on her lips. She had no idea what he was thinking, wasn't sure she wanted to know, because whatever it was, it looked ominous. Perhaps talking about it wasn't such a great idea. Callie lifted her glass. "Do you want a drink?" He shook his head and she took a sip herself. The water did nothing to ease the sudden dryness in her throat.

He studied her face, his own a mask of grim determination. "Marry me."

Seven

Callie almost choked as she swallowed. She took a deep, gasping breath and put down her glass. "I think you misheard me. I said, 'do you want a drink,' not, 'I love you and want to spend my life with you.'"

One side of his mouth twitched upward. "I heard you." The half smile disappeared. He shoved his fists into the pockets of his black pants.

"Then maybe I misheard *you*."

He shook his head. "I didn't mention love or wanting to spend a lifetime together, either. I presented the obvious solution to your dilemma, which is for us to get married. Surely you expected no less."

Her words from their first meeting came back to her as she met Nick's gaze: "If you're choosing between bad company and loneliness, choose the latter." His eyes widened and she pushed on. "So, flattering as your heartfelt proposal is, I don't think the best solution for my dilemma is to create an entirely new set of problems. I compromised once before. I won't do it again. My expectations don't include having any more to do with you than I have to. And given that we're business partners as well as parents-to-be, I'm confident I'll have more than my fill."

Some of the tension eased from his stance, but the lines across his forehead deepened. "You're saying no?"

She almost smiled. Had he really thought she might say yes? "Absolutely, I'm saying no. When—if—I get married, I have certain requirements."

His eyebrows lifted. "I don't meet them?"

"For starters, men who bulldoze their way to getting what they want have never really done it for me."

"Bulldoze?" He looked as though he might argue with that.

She held his gaze. "Bulldoze, steamroll, take your pick. Like you did with my business."

"I try to find the most efficient way of tackling my problems," he said quietly.

"Regardless of who's in your way?"

Something shifted in the green depths of his eyes. "I always take into account who's in my way."

Right now they were very much in each other's way, standing inches apart. Callie's pulse leapt traitorously. There were some things that she didn't doubt would be good between them, at least in the short term.

She took a step back. "I really need to get ready for this dinner."

"Go ahead," he said easily.

"But—"

"I'll wait for you." He picked up the hotel's complimentary newspaper from the table.

She looked into his eyes, saw the implacability, and for a moment thought she saw something else too, something like—not vulnerability—but perhaps need, as though this really was important to him.

Sighing, Callie found her clothes for the evening and took them into the bathroom. She showered, keeping her cut hand outside the curtain, and did her very best to shut out thoughts of Nick; but that was easier said than done when she was standing naked under a stream of hot water and far too aware that he was on the other side of the door. Even if he was engrossed in the paper.

She had just finished drying herself when his deep voice carried through the door. "You don't think marriage and a stable family life is the best way to raise a child?"

So much for reading the paper. "I definitely think that." She reached for her underwear and stepped quickly into it. "If the marriage is happy."

"It puts in place the best structure for raising a child." His voice through the door was calm and measured.

Callie was anything but. "Best in the right circumstances." She slipped her dress over her head, smoothed it over her hips. "These aren't them."

"A child needs two parents."

Callie turned and rested her forehead on the door. "Who love each other." This was hurting. As if he could read her thoughts he was raising all the arguments and insecurities that circled as she tried to sleep at night. She straightened and opened the door. He was close, his forearm raised above his head as he leaned against the door frame. His jacket hung open and her gaze caught on the small V of masculine skin revealed by the undone top button of his shirt.

She dragged her gaze upward. "Supposedly, it takes a whole village to raise a child. That doesn't mean it's a good idea to marry the baker, and the blacksmith and the woman who takes in laundry."

"People can grow to love each other." He said thoughtfully, as though considering the concept.

Callie couldn't fathom anything in those deep green eyes, and yet they held her, slowed the beating of her heart. "What are you saying?"

He shook his head, breaking the contact of his gaze. "I'm saying marry me. I want the child to have my name."

The hollowness swelled within her and she took a step back, turned to the counter and busied herself looking in her makeup bag. "No."

"Think about it."

"I just did."

Nick sighed. "Then think some more. But regardless of when or…if you marry me, I'll provide whatever you need." He spoke to her back. "But in return I want to know that you're not going to try to shut me out. That you'll let me be the best father to our child that I can."

She set her mascara and lipstick on the counter and turned back to him. She wasn't going to be drawn in on the marriage issue, but she could assure him on some points at least.

"Three things. First—" she held up one finger "—I wouldn't try to shut you out. I wouldn't do that to our child. He'll need and want contact with his father. I know that."

"He? What did the doctor tell you?" The question was sharp and very interested.

"Not that. I'm only ten weeks, and they won't be able to tell the sex till I have a scan around twenty. But I can't keep calling it, 'it.'" She smoothed a hand over her still-almost-flat stomach. "Sometimes I think *she*."

"She," he said abruptly. "She's a girl." He looked as though he regretted the words as soon as they were out of his mouth. His gaze slid away from her.

"Why do you say that?"

He lifted one shoulder. "Devil's advocate," he said lightly, then nodded, the movement abrupt. "Go on."

"Second," she said as she cleared a circle on the steam-dampened mirror with a hand towel. "I play fair." Even in the mirror she could read the skepticism in his eyes. "Ask Jason." She leaned toward the glass and brushed smoky eye shadow over her eyelids.

"I'd rather not ask Jason about you."

It was small consolation that, if this was messy for her, it was at least as messy for him. "Do he and Melody know?"

"No."

She swept on her mascara. "Why not?"

"I haven't seen much of them lately. Besides, I didn't think they needed to know. Not yet anyway."

Callie put the mascara back in her bag. "How will Melody take the news?" This was the woman who thought she'd been trying to cling to Jason. And now Callie was having her brother's baby.

"Mel's swept up with her own pregnancy. Her first thought will probably be, great, a cousin for my child."

"Extended, divided families. It promises to be so much fun." Callie paused. "Is she still worried about me and Jason?" She stretched her lips and carefully applied plum-colored lipstick.

"No."

She turned away from the mirror and met his gaze directly, tried to read his thoughts. "Are you?"

His gaze lingered for a moment on her lips. "It was never about what I thought. And the third thing?"

He hadn't answered her question, but Callie let it pass. She wasn't sure she wanted to know his answer. "The third thing," she tried to remember what it had been as she packed her cosmetics back into her bag and closed it. "You own half of my business. Something to do with control and leverage, if I remember correctly." He had the power to do her a lot of damage.

The light in Nick's eyes changed. "I'd forgotten."

It was reassuring that he had. He wasn't already looking at this as a battle and assessing potential weapons.

Callie opened the bathroom door wider and stepped past him, doing her best to ignore the gaze that swept her from head to toe. She reached into the closet for her shoes—too high, but gorgeous black patent leather evening sandals. She was about to slip them onto her feet when she remembered her toenails. She glanced at the bedside clock. There was still time.

Sitting on her bed, she shook a bottle of nail polish and watched as Nick paced the room. He picked up a menu for the hotel restaurant, glanced over it before dropping it back down and turning to her. "You claimed at the awards dinner that a rumor of pregnancy would be bad for your business. How will the reality affect it?"

She shook the small bottle more vigorously. "I'll manage it."

"How?"

"I don't know yet." The questions put her on the

spot. He was doing it again, getting way ahead of her and what she was ready to deal with. "Whatever it is, I'll manage. It's what I do."

"I'll help."

That she was so ready to believe him should probably worry her. It was his business too, she reminded herself. He was only protecting his investment. But she didn't doubt that, for some things at least, he would be in her corner. The even more worrying thought was that he would be a good man to have there. "Thanks," she said, and meant it.

Silence settled over them. Callie loosened the lid of the bottle and looked at her toes. Nick's dark shoes appeared in her line of sight. "If you really want to help, you could do this for me." She held up the nail polish.

Showing neither surprise nor reluctance, Nick took the bottle from her and sat on the opposite bed. "Give me your foot." She should have known better than to hope that her request might scare him off.

Callie was suddenly the reluctant one. "Do you know what you're doing?"

He smiled. "It's been a while, but Mel used to get me to help her when she was younger." He shrugged. "I have steady hands." Callie watched those steady hands unscrew the lid. "How will your family take the news?" he asked, holding out a hand for her foot.

She placed her heel into the cradle of his palm and watched, fascinated, as, holding the delicate brush in large fingers, he brushed on an even stroke of glistening plum polish.

"You do have family?" He glanced up before applying another stroke.

She nodded. "A mother."

"That's all?" He moved to her next toe.

"Obviously I have or had a father, but I've never met him." She'd had a good childhood, but knew she didn't want that same vague sense of something missing, of abandonment, for her child.

It seemed a long time before he spoke again. "You've told your mother?"

"Not yet."

"It might be easier to break it to her along with the news of our engagement."

She met his gaze. "Or not."

He nodded, but somehow it didn't seem to mean agreement.

"How will she take it?"

"She has no grounds for criticism, if that's what you mean." In fact, Callie, who'd tried so hard to be different from her free-spirited mother, had instead followed right along in her careless footsteps in accidentally getting pregnant.

Nick finished another toe and looked up again. Concern softened his gaze. "I meant, will you get support from her?"

"Yes. If I ask." And it was the asking that would be the hard part. Asking, that Callie saw as a sign of not being able to cope on her own. A sign that she'd failed. Stupid really, because Gypsy would only want to help, would delight in a grandchild—one she could lavish her affection on when she breezed into the country. "What about your family?"

He shrugged as though he hadn't given it any thought. And yet he'd wondered about her family's reaction. "So long as they're allowed to feel the child is part of the family, they'll be happy."

He made it sound so simple.

Callie withdrew her finished foot from his clasp and paused before she lifted her other one, settled it into the hand that rested, waiting, on his thigh. He met her gaze over her leg, his green eyes soft. For a few moments it was as though everything would be all right, that between them they could make it so.

"And you?" That gaze assessed her closely. "Are you okay with being a single mother?"

Callie took a deep breath. "I think life is trying to tell me that I can't plan it all out. I wanted to do things the right way—stable relationship, love, marriage, then kids."

For long seconds neither of them spoke. Nick of the steady hands painted her toenails. "Love, marriage and kids. That's what you thought you were getting with Jason?" He finished a toe and looked up, intent.

"Yes. I'd thought, hoped, that was where we were going. But I guess I was projecting my fantasy ideals onto him. And he was comfortable with the situation— till a better offer came along."

Nick's fingers stilled. "Are you suggesting he married Melody for—"

"I'm not suggesting anything. Jason loves her in a way he never loved me." He'd kindly told her that himself. "I just didn't realize how much more was possible than what we had." She paused, felt the hollowness inside. "I won't settle for less a second time."

Nick replaced the cap on the bottle and his hand came to rest on the top of her foot, warm and strong, fingers curving around it. "And marrying me would be settling for less?"

"You know it would. I want the real thing, and I don't want to deny either of us the chance of finding it."

He lifted her foot, blew gently on the nails before lowering it back to his leg. "What if there is no real thing?"

The warm breath, the gesture, disconcerted her, she scrambled for thought. "There is." There had to be.

"You may never find it."

Callie pulled her foot from his hand, placed it firmly on the floor. "I know that's a possibility." And at almost thirty the possibility seemed very real. "But it's better than the certainty that if we tie each other up in a marriage we'll never find it. Or it'll be really messy if one of us does. Besides, you're not in the market for any kind of commitment."

"I can commit."

She held his gaze. "Professionally and financially, sure. But not personally or emotionally. I did some research. You've been romantically linked to numerous beautiful women. Nothing has stuck. And you're forgetting I know about Angelina, I remember you celebrating the end of a relationship that was looking like too much commitment."

Nick was silent for a long time. He was looking at her, but not really seeing her.

"That was different."

With that nonargument, a weight settled in the air. Callie glanced at her toes, wiggled them a little. "Good job on the nail polish. I could probably get you some regular clients."

"Don't you dare tell a soul," he growled, but he was smiling and she remembered how and why she'd been so attracted to him that first night. His smile did something wonderful to his face. "I hope our baby gets your smile." The words slipped out.

His gaze sharpened on her, then softened and lingered. "And your eyes."

He liked her eyes? Startled by the warmth that simple statement generated, Callie stood. She needed to remain neutral toward him, needed to retain her independence from him. "I should get going." She slid her feet carefully into her open-toe sandals.

Nick stood too. "I'll walk you down."

As they passed the still open wardrobe door, Callie glanced critically at her reflection in the full-length mirror. She lifted a hand to her hair. She'd left it out, curling softly around her face. If she'd been able to get an appointment—

"It looks beautiful. *You* look beautiful." Nick fingered one of the curls, his knuckle brushing against her neck igniting her skin.

She met his gaze in the mirror. "What if I say yes?"

"Then we'll get married."

"And make each other miserable."

A hint of a smile touched his face. "Perhaps." He paused, the smile faded and his mouth turned serious. He shifted his hand to her shoulder, turned her toward him. "You deserve to be happy. I would find ways to not to make you miserable."

"That would have sounded good in the marriage vows. I'll find ways to not make you miserable." Callie tried to make light of the situation, but still neither of them moved. A connection shimmered in the air between them, slowing her heartbeat to a heavy, anticipatory thump.

Her phone rang in her evening bag, shrill and abrupt. Once then twice. Blinking, Callie found it and glanced at the caller ID. "Marc, how's it going?"

As Marc spoke, she exhaled heavily, her thoughts firmly back in reality. "Of course you have to go home. Don't worry about the festival, I'll sort it out." She listened a little longer, then cut in. "I meant it when I said don't worry. Just get yourself home as quickly as you can."

She shut off her phone and looked at Nick, who'd moved away, but was watching her. "Marc's your side-kick at Ivy Cottage?"

She nodded, still processing the news he'd delivered. "He's been at Cypress Rise. I had him organizing the Jazz and Art festival."

"And?" Nick probed gently.

"His sister's been in a car crash. She's in a coma." The woman Callie had met only a few times had been so vivacious it was impossible to imagine her lying still and injured in a hospital bed.

"Does he need help getting home?" Nick's concern was immediate. "Brunicadi Investments has a jet that's available."

Callie shook her head and started toward her hotel room door. "He's booked on the next flight out, and is already on his way to the airport."

Nick opened the door for her. "Good."

She waited for him in the corridor. "It does leave a problem with the festival."

His gaze sharpened. "Who'll cover it now?"

They walked toward the elevators. "That's the problem. Aside from me there isn't anyone else. Before he left, Jason used to do a lot of these sorts of things. If he's available to help, I guess he could step in. But he would still have to liaise with me."

Nick shook his head.

So he still doubted her. And it hurt. "Don't you think the festival is more important than these insecurities? Heck, we can have a third person present during all contact if that makes it any easier."

He shook his head again. "Jason's out of the country."

"Oh." It hadn't been concern over her and Jason. At least not entirely. "Then I'm the only other person who can take over." She watched him closely as they waited for an elevator to arrive. She'd put Marc in charge of the day in an effort to minimize her contact with the winery and Melody. But she really was the only one who could step in now, the only other person who'd had involvement with the caterers, artists, performers and security.

He saw her dilemma. Knew it, because he'd created it.

"I know it goes against what we agreed—what you demanded I agree to—but that really wasn't necessary in the first place. For the winery's sake, and for the sake of the teenage shelter, we need to do it right and do it well."

The elevator arrived and they stepped in. "I'll drive you." There was no hesitation, no reluctance in his calm response.

Did that mean he trusted her? And should she want that trust as much as she did? "I don't want to put you to any trouble." She matched his calmness, but already her thoughts were torn between cataloging what still needed to be done in the run-up to the weekend, and how she would juggle the work on her desk back home; and underneath all that ran a ripple of anxiety about what it would be like to be on his territory.

"It's no trouble. I promised Mel I'd be around this week."

The ripple increased. "You're helping out at the festival?"

"You sound surprised."

"I hadn't realized, that's all. Doing what?"

"General drudge work, as far as I can tell. She's making all the family come and help." One side of his mouth kicked up in a grin as the elevator came to a halt. "So when do you want to go?"

This was happening too fast, but she knew it had to. "Early tomorrow morning I guess," she said hesitantly. "I'd like to get there in time to put in a full day."

"You're not needed here?"

She shook her head. "This dinner is the last thing I have to be here for."

"I'll pick you up at six then."

Suddenly, the trip in the car with him, spending days on his territory seemed like a very bad idea. He confused her, and confused her senses.

They stepped into the foyer. In a bar area off the far side of the marbled room, several of the people she was meeting for dinner stood clustered together, sipping cocktails.

The adjacent elevator doors opened, and Len Joseph, whose company was one of the principal conference sponsors, stepped out. A smile spread across his lined face as he saw Callie and Nick. "Wonderful that you could join us for dinner." He clapped Nick on the shoulder.

Callie's heart sank. Yet another opportunity for Nick to intrude in her life, a further confusing of the lines. And she couldn't even accuse him of bulldozing when the opportunity was handed to him on a plate.

"Thanks, Len." Nick glanced at Callie. "But I can't tonight."

"Sorry to hear that. Some other time." Len headed for the group of dinner guests.

She looked at Nick. "Thanks."

"For not bulldozing?"

"Something like that."

He smiled and Callie dragged her gaze away to look at the group Len had joined. Their presence anchored her and reminded her what she was doing here and who she was, Callie Jamieson, PR professional. She knew how to be that woman. All she had to do was focus on that and do her job. The rest, the confusing stuff—her pregnancy and more specifically her relationship with Nick—she could deal with later.

"The pregnancy changes everything, Callie." He spoke close to her ear. "You're having my baby," he said as though he'd read her thoughts. "Whether you like it or not, and even before you agree to marry me that makes you a part of my family. The two can't be separated."

Eight

Still mulling over his parting words, Callie stood under the hotel's portico the next morning, watching the Sydney street come to life. From his cool non-offer of marriage, she'd been catapulted into the prospect of days spent in Nick's company, with all the things they'd said—and done—hanging between them.

Five minutes ahead of time, a black Range Rover eased to a stop in front of her. Nick nodded a greeting as he got out and opened her door. Wearing snug jeans that were faded just a little, and a black polo shirt, he looked more casual than she'd yet seen him. Casual, yet no less potent. She had to pass close to him to get into the car, and remembered of all things, the warm caress of his breath on her bare toes. She caught his scent, clean and masculine, as she climbed into the deep beige seat. He shut her door, leaving her with a feeling similar to what she got when she strapped herself into the seat of a rollercoaster. Suddenly, when it was too late to back out, there was an overwhelming uncertainty as to whether this wasn't a very bad idea.

He stowed her bag in the back, climbed in beside her then pulled smoothly away. Definitely too late now. "You've been in touch with Marc this morning? How's his sister?" he asked as he passed her a paper bakery bag. All business, she noted, though his concern was genuine.

"Yes. He got home all right, but there's no change in his sister's condition." And she was almost equally surprised when she looked inside the bag and saw a cream cheese bagel and a date scone. Beside her, in the cup holders, sat two bottles of mineral water.

"And nothing else we can do for him or his family?"

"Not at this stage. I've told him to take as much time as he needs off work." She watched to gauge his response, but if she was expecting any protest at the likely effect on her bottom line, she didn't get it. Nick nodded his agreement. "Is this for me?" She lifted up the bag.

"I didn't know if you'd have had time for breakfast. We can stop somewhere along the way, once we get out of the city, but that's—" he pointed at the bag "—just in case."

Did he know that she was almost constantly hungry? The pregnancy book she had bought informed her that the baby, at just under three months, was only a couple of inches long. How did something that size have such a profound affect on her appetite? "Thank you." She broke a corner off the scone, light and buttery and still warm from the oven, and popped it into her mouth.

"How was your dinner?"

"Good." She paused. "You could have come if you'd wanted to."

His laughter was the last thing she expected, filling the interior of the car with its warmth and surprising a laugh out of her too. "All right," she admitted, "I was relieved when you turned the invitation down."

They lapsed into silence. Callie sought for something to say. She glanced across at him. Her gaze caught on his hands, strong and capable on the steering wheel, took in the light covering of hair on tanned forearms. The urge to touch her fingertips to those arms to see how the play of muscle would feel caught her by surprise. She swallowed and looked resolutely out the windshield.

Uncomfortable in the confined space, hyperaware of his presence and Nick's nearness, Callie made phone calls to keep herself occupied, following up on Marc's arrangements, satisfying herself that everything was under control.

Nick remained silent, keeping any feelings on her impending presence at Cypress Rise to himself. Outside, the vast summer-browned countryside slid by.

She finished a phone call with the caterers and looked across at him. "Does Melody know I'm coming?"

He nodded.

"And she's okay with it?"

"She understands why you need to come." After a pause, he added. "She never knew I'd told you to cut the contact. She had asked me to check you out, so to speak. After which, all I told her was that she didn't have anything to worry about."

"I don't understand how someone like Melody, who would appear to have it all, gets to be so insecure."

"A woman like you wouldn't."

"What's that supposed to mean?" Callie bristled.

Nick flicked a glance in her direction. "It's a compliment. You're strong."

"Oh." He thought she was strong? He had no inkling of her uncertainties, her fears of being inadequate for the things ahead of her.

"Have you always protected her?"

He shot her another glance, took his time answering. "I guess so. Because of the gap in our ages, in some ways I was more like a father to her. Our own father wasn't around that much."

"Where was he?"

"He was heavily involved in his work."

"And your mother?"

Nick paused, this one even longer than the last. "Died when Melody was three."

Callie hid her shock at the thought. Nick could only have been thirteen. Her heart ached for the boy he'd been, and for Melody too.

"Rosa, my grandmother, stepped into the breach," he continued. "We never wanted for anything."

Callie studied his profile as he pulled out and passed a tractor towing hay-baling equipment. He looked so strong, and he was strong—not letting himself need anyone—but it had come at a price.

"Not wanting for anything didn't mean you weren't hurting."

He gave a slight shake of his head. "We were okay. It made us closer at the time."

"And you're still close?"

"We're family." He said it as though that simple statement answered everything. And last night he'd said she was now a part of that family. "Mel's been better the last few years. Along with the success of the winery, her self-confidence has grown. She's intelligent and savvy. But those days cast a long shadow, and she's always been a little insecure."

And how had those days affected Nick? Clearly, they'd made him protective of his sister; but were they, combined with his girlfriend's betrayal, behind his reluctance to commit emotionally? Was that how he was able to keep marriage as a solution to a problem, without offering anything of himself?

"Mel's okay now. She's partially blaming hormones for her concerns over you."

There were two of them dealing with that particular issue. Callie was aware of the exaggerated peaks and troughs of her moods and emotional responses to things that wouldn't usually bother her, like sappy television commercials, like the times when a perceived gentleness in Nick could make her want to throw away her principles as she threw herself into his arms. "When does Jason get back?" And how would that affect the mix?

"Do you want him to be there?" Nick's gaze stayed trained on the road, but she knew his attention was on her.

Callie considered the question. "I haven't spoken to him since he sold out to you. So there are some things I'd like to say to him." She grinned. "But it's probably for the best if I don't."

"He's in California. He's due back in just over a week."

The subject sat uneasily between them. She wanted Nick at least to think better of her than his sister did, but he revealed so little of what he really thought. Maybe that was for the best, because if someone knew him and grew to care for him too much, that person would ultimately be the one who got hurt.

She had thought that she would be stronger after

what had happened with Jason, that she would develop a tougher outer shell. But Nick had already shown her the cracks in that shell. She would lean on him, if he let her, like at the hospital. And she couldn't afford to lean.

They drove through vine-covered land rich with the greens and browns of late summer. "It's beautiful here." Nonchalant, uninvolved. She could do it.

"Do you want to go to the house first, or straight to the winery?"

"The winery, thanks. I have a feeling it's going to be a big day."

A few miles farther along, Nick swung the car off the road and drove through an imposing gateway set in a low, stone wall, and lettered with the flowing logo for Cypress Rise Wines. They followed a side road that took them behind the public reception area used for wine tastings, and then around the back. She undid her seat belt as they eased to a stop, and they got out.

Nick led the way to a simple office building. Off to one side, stainless steel vats and stairways rose from the ground. He pushed open a door and stepped back for her to precede him inside.

Melody sat at a desk, computer monitor in front of her, neat piles of paper stacked on her left. This was the woman who'd thought Callie was trying to sabotage her marriage. Callie wasn't sure whether she should still feel angry about that, or just sorry for her. Melody looked up, and at the sight of Callie a slight flush rose up her face. She stood and came around to meet them. "I'm so glad you could make it. How's Marc's sister?" There was a wariness in her eyes. Eyes that Callie saw now were the same green as Nick's.

"She's stable, but other than that there's no change."

"We were so sorry to hear about her accident. We don't know her, of course, but all the staff were enjoying working with Marc. He had such a great sense of humor. We've sent her some flowers. Irises and daisies..." She trailed off.

Melody was definitely babbling, and she'd never struck Callie as a babbler before; so that meant Callie, and whatever lay between them, was making her nervous. A quagmire spread before her: did she mention the wedding, the honeymoon, ask after Jason? Questions that, with another client, would have been no more than polite. "I imagine things are really heating up here. Is there anything pressing we need to address?"

"Yes." Mel's face relaxed. Getting straight to business obviously suited her fine. "There's an interview scheduled with a local radio station in half an hour. It was supposed to be tomorrow, but they brought it forward. I hate that sort of thing, and Marc was going to do it."

"Did he get any notes on the questions they plan on asking?"

"Yes." Mel rummaged on her desk, picked up a sheet of printed paper and held it out gratefully to Callie. Marc's neat handwriting lined the margins and the spaces between the questions. "Have you got time to run through this with me?"

"I'll do anything you want, if it means I don't have to do that interview."

They started going through the questions together, both thoroughly professional, even if the interaction lacked ease or warmth. At the sound of Nick clearing his throat they looked up. He stood at the door. "I'll see you both later."

Callie nodded. Melody uttered a small "Oh". Then recovered. "Okay."

The door swung shut behind him, his absence leaving a strange vacuum. Had Melody wanted to call him back too?

But any doubts Callie had about the potential for uneasiness between them turned out to be unnecessary. There was so much to do that there was no time for awkwardness. Jason had always been the main contact between Ivy Cottage and the vineyard, and then Marc; but Callie had kept herself up-to-date and had occasionally dealt with Melody, and they'd always worked well together. It was no different today, professionally speaking. Occasionally Callie caught Melody looking at her, her glance quick and curious.

It was several rushed hours later before Nick came back through the door. "Lunch? Rosa's waiting."

"You go ahead," Melody said, "I brought lunch to have here. I've got a phone call to make."

"You're sure?" Nick asked.

Melody's glance darted between Nick and Callie. "Positive." Callie figured she planned to phone Jason.

Nick shrugged and held the door open. She passed by him and they walked toward his vehicle. "How did it go this morning?" he asked.

"Well. Everything's on target. We got a lot done. Though the big stuff was already sorted. It's really only tying up the details over the next couple of days. But there are more than enough of them."

He nodded as he helped her into the car. "You're not too tired?"

She turned in her seat and met his gaze, didn't want the closeness she felt at his concern, didn't want special treatment. "I'm not an invalid."

"Just busy," he said calmly, "and pregnant. And you

had a late night and an early start. It wasn't an unreasonable question." He shut her door gently, crossed in front of the car to get in behind the wheel.

"Sorry. I'm fine." Callie backed down. "Thanks for asking." She had to make this work, had to stop herself reacting—correction, overreacting—to him.

His knowing eyes didn't conceal the flash of humor as he glanced at her.

He pulled away from the winery and back onto the main road, then turned off again a few miles farther along.

A couple of minutes later he slowed and turned again, this time into a cypress-lined driveway. As the road wound its way up a hill, the trees gave way to reveal a sprawling Mediterranean-style villa.

"This is home?"

"I divide my time between here and my apartment in Sydney. I prefer it here, but the business dictates I spend a fair amount of time where I'm accessible for meetings and close to the airport." He looked out the window, scanning the surrounding countryside. "My family has lived in this area for three generations." He glanced at her, his green eyes enigmatic. "Four soon, I guess."

She supposed he could call it that. Though how much time their child got to spend here remained to be seen. Or perhaps he was referring only to Jason and Melody's child.

He slowed to a halt and got out. Before she'd even finished unbuckling her belt he had opened her door. A wave of heat washed into the cool interior. Nick's face was level with hers. Her gaze lighted on his lips. And the heat intensified. She remembered too well kissing those full lips. For a moment she thought of kissing them once again, of tasting him. Quickly averting her gaze, she blamed errant hormones for the passing temptation.

"I'm glad Melody won't be here," he said as he held out his hand.

Unresisting, Callie placed her hand in his. "Why?" she stepped down from the car. Nick didn't move, didn't release his clasp. They stood mere inches apart. Could he feel the way he made her pulse race?

He looked toward the house. "It's best we meet Rosa on our own."

Did he even know he was still holding her hand, his clasp warm and sure, gently possessive? "You're making her sound scary. Does she bite?" Callie extricated her hand. She needed to think straight.

"No. And she's not scary." He turned back. "But I should warn you about her."

Her gaze was caught by the dark lashes fringing those deep green eyes. He was still so close, so captivating. She need only lift her hand to touch him again. "Warn me?" She tried to keep her voice light. But it obviously wasn't only his grandmother someone needed to warn her away from, because she didn't seem able to heed her own warnings not to let herself feel anything for him.

Nick searched her gaze before speaking. "Sometimes she *knows* things, or thinks she does." The words seemed drawn reluctantly from him.

Callie tried to read in his eyes the meaning of the emphasis he'd placed on the word *know*. "What sort of things?"

"Usually, only things to do with family." A slight frown creased his brow.

She wanted to touch her fingertips to his forehead, to smooth away the lines. She swallowed. "Like what?"

"Like, who's calling when the phone rings. Or she'll suddenly decide to make extra cannelloni for dinner, and then friends drop in on the spur of the moment. Coincidental things, but uncanny all the same." His gaze held hers—a hint of apology in it—and he took a deep breath. "Pregnancy—the expansion of the Brunicadi clan—is her specialty."

They both looked toward the house just as the enormous front door swung open. "Dominic." A plump, gray-haired woman dressed in head-to-toe black, her face creasing into a smile, bustled toward them.

"Rosa," he greeted her.

She kissed Nick on both cheeks before enfolding him in an embrace. Then she turned to Callie, and before Nick had even finished introducing them had kissed her twice too. Still holding Callie's shoulders, she stepped back and surveyed her. Her eyes narrowed for a moment. "Come inside. Lunch is ready. I've made gnocchi."

As they walked into the house she glanced twice more at Callie.

They were in the cool, spacious kitchen, filled with the aromas of cooking, when Rosa looked again at Callie then turned to Nick. "Why didn't you tell me?"

Surely she couldn't have guessed already. Callie glanced at Nick, who had tilted his head inquiringly, as though he didn't know what his grandmother was asking. But Callie was suddenly certain that everybody knew what was being asked.

"The *bambina*."

He glanced at Callie, gave a resigned shrug. "We haven't told anyone, Rosa. You're the first to know." He almost made it sound like they were a couple who planned on sharing their news with friends and family.

The old woman rounded on Callie, a smile crinkling her already well-wrinkled face. "When is the *bambina* due? You need to eat more, you're too skinny." She grabbed Callie's hand, her grip surprisingly firm, and pulled her toward an expansive table.

She had Callie sitting with an enormous bowl of gnocchi in an aromatic sauce in front of her before she'd had time to gather her breath. "I bought pink wool last week. Now I know why." Another Brunicadi certain she was having a girl. Callie glanced at Nick.

But he was looking at his grandmother. "It's early days, Rosa," he cautioned.

"Paah! You think these things can change halfway through," she said scathingly. "It's a girl. I'll start knitting this afternoon." Rosa scarcely paused. "When is the wedding? I'm not having Melody tell me I need another new dress. She's too wasteful, that one."

Nick looked at her, giving her a chance to change her mind before he gave Rosa the bad news. Callie shook her head.

"We're not getting married," he said, and she was grateful for the certainty of that statement, at least in front of his family.

Rosa sat up straighter. "No grandson of mine will live in sin."

"We're not going to live together." His tone was firm but resigned. He obviously knew what was coming.

Rosa's chair scraped across the terra-cotta floor tiles as she pushed it back from the table and stood. "Come," she barked the order at Nick. Then she nodded sympathetically at Callie. "I will talk to him. *Un momento, per favore.*"

"But—"

Nick touched a hand to Callie's shoulder and shook his head to silence her protest, then stood and followed his grandmother to a door leading off the kitchen. Just before he passed through it, he turned back. "Her bark is worse than her bite," he said in a low voice, "but it's loud all the same."

"You told me she didn't bite at all."

He was smiling as he closed the door behind him. The slab of solid wood did little to disguise the tirade of angry Italian coming from the other side of it. Callie wasn't sure whether to feel sorry for him or to laugh.

But her conscience would only let her sit there for so long while he took all the blame for the fact that there would be no wedding. She stood and followed them, pushed open the door to see Rosa, who scarcely came up to Nick's shoulders, with a finger in his chest. They both looked at her, and Rosa's diatribe halted.

"Mrs. Brunicadi—"

"Rosa," the older woman quickly interrupted.

"Nick asked me to marry him." A strong hand came to rest on her shoulder. She looked across at Nick, who'd come to stand beside her, caught the small shake of his head and ignored it. "It's not what I want," she said as she looked back at Rosa.

"Of course it is."

"No. It's not," she said quietly, aware of two pairs of surprised eyes on her.

Rosa harrumphed, glared for a while longer at Nick, then, with an air of injured dignity, went back into the kitchen.

Nick stood in front of her, his head tilted to one side, his green eyes curious. "I don't think anyone's ever done that before. Tried to defend me to Rosa." A half smile tilted his lips. "You didn't have to."

"It seemed only fair. Besides, I get to leave after the end of the festival. Escape any more fallout."

The smile turned rueful. "She'll come around. But she needed to rant, to get it off her chest."

With one reassuring hand at the small of her back, he guided her back to the table, and unperturbed, waited for her to sit. They ate in relative companionability, though every now and then Rosa muttered to herself in Italian, and either frowned at Nick or looked pityingly at Callie. And Callie knew that she still thought it was Nick's fault there would be no wedding, that no woman in her right mind would turn down his offer of marriage. It was easy to see why she thought that way.

Nick watched Callie swallow the last of her gnocchi and edge her bowl away. "I'll show you the guest cottage." As seductive as watching her eat was, he needed to get her away from Rosa, who couldn't be counted on to forbear on the subject of marriage much longer. And while he wanted Callie to come to accept that marrying him was the best option, she needed space to do that, not badgering.

She paused as they rounded a bend in the path. "Cottage?" she challenged with a grin and a glint in her eyes. That grin was its own version of sunshine and temptation. Shaking her head, she kept walking toward the house that was a smaller version of the family home.

Nick held open the door that led into a spacious and light-filled interior furnished in creams and neutrals.

She trailed behind him as he showed her the bedroom, its broad, high bed piled with pillows, and the marble bathroom with its deep spa bath.

Back in the living room a ceiling fan spun lazily above them, barely moving the warm air. Nick leaned against a door frame, watching her and waiting for her reaction as she crossed to the wide windows and looked out over distant rows of green vines stretching across the hillsides. She turned. "It's beautiful here," she said, her expression enchanting.

She turned back to the window. "It's so peaceful. It quiets something inside. Gives a perspective that makes you believe everything will be okay."

That was how he'd always felt coming here. Cypress Rise was good for his soul. And she felt it too. That thought troubled him almost as much as it pleased him. He needed her to like it here. He didn't need to feel that she belonged. That she, too, might be good for his soul. Because his soul was just fine without her.

He stepped back. "Whenever you're ready I'll take you back to the vineyard office."

"I'm ready now."

In his car again, she looked at him. "I can't see that Melody's going to be thrilled at the prospect of me having your baby."

He reached across, touched his hand to her shoulder. "It's our business, Callie. Not anyone else's." He put his hand back on the wheel. "Though they'll definitely try to make it so. Still, you don't need to worry at the moment. Rosa won't tell anyone about the pregnancy yet, although we won't be able to stop her from knitting."

"When will you tell Melody?"

"Maybe after the festival, when she doesn't have so much on her mind. She'll know you better by then. You two will like each other."

"Is that another Brunicadi prediction?"

"No. This is a knowledge of people. Of Melody and of you."

"You don't really know me."

"I know you better than you think, better than you want to believe."

Nine

Melody was on the phone as Callie walked into the office. The remnants of a salad-filled sandwich and an apple core lay on a plate in front of her. A second phone on her desk was ringing. Callie gestured toward it and Melody nodded for her to pick it up. Odds were it would be about the festival.

"Cypress Rise."

"Darling. I forgot to say—"

"Jason?" Funny, a part of her observed, how the sound of his voice did nothing to her. She was still annoyed at him. But it was an unemotional kind of annoyed.

"Callie." The pause was long. "I've been meaning to get in touch with you to explain—"

There were no explanations she needed or wanted from him. "I assume you want Melody." She lowered the phone and held it out.

As Melody finished the call she was on, Callie passed over the phone, busied herself in paperwork, humming quietly to drown out whatever Melody was saying. And when Melody hung up they picked up where they had left off before Callie had gone for lunch.

The afternoon was just as busy as the morning. They spent time with the vineyard staff, as well as with artists and musicians arranging and rearranging details of the weekend. There were the usual last-minute hitches and panics, but by six o'clock Callie was confident everything was under control. The to-do list for the rest of the week was full but manageable.

Melody sat back in her chair and breathed a heavy sigh. "We should go up to the house. Rosa expects everyone to eat dinner together." She patted her faintly rounded stomach. "And I'm finding I have to eat really regularly anyway. This little boy is doing terrible things to my appetite. I'm going to be the size of a house by the time he comes." Melody's jaw dropped and the hand that had rested on her stomach suddenly clapped over her mouth.

Did Melody think Callie didn't know about the baby? "I heard a whisper at the wedding. It's wonderful news." Callie tried to put her at ease. "I haven't congratulated you and Jason yet—" *because your brother forbade me to talk to either of you* "—but I wish you all the best with your pregnancy. I'm sure you'll be wonderful parents." She meant every word, didn't feel any of that sense of inadequacy she had when she'd first heard about their pregnancy.

She really had moved on. And that was due in part to Nick. For better or worse, he'd presented her with enough issues in her own life that she didn't have the time or energy to spare to be anxious about anyone else's life.

Melody's smile was a mix of relief and pride. "I didn't know whether… How you'd… If…" She tripped over her words, her eyes wide in her delicate face. Callie could suddenly see why Jason had fallen for her. Not only was she beautiful and sweet, but there was a fragility about her that Jason would want to protect. She would let him be the big, strong man he pictured himself as. Callie had never let him be that for her.

She didn't want that in a man. She wanted a partner. She thought of Nick, who was a partner in the commercial sense. She mentally exchanged the word "partner" for "equal," and realized he was that too.

"I'm thrilled for you," said Callie, dragging her thoughts back to safe ground. "Just be careful you don't let the stress of the festival get to you. Take all the rest you need to. Pass whatever you don't want to deal with over to me." Heck, Melody was even bringing out Callie's protective instincts. She almost laughed at the concept—had forgotten for a while that she was pregnant too.

"Thank you." Mel picked up a glass paperweight and turned it in her fingers. The gesture reminded Callie of Nick. "There's something else I wanted to discuss with you."

Callie thought she knew what was coming, and if, as she suspected, it was anything to do with Jason, or Melody's doubt, she'd really rather not have this conversation. At the sound of a tap on the door they looked around—Callie with relief—to see Nick.

His gaze went to Callie, assessing, then flicked to his sister. Apparently satisfied with what he saw, he spoke. "Rosa's waiting for you both."

He held the door open for them. Melody went out first,

Callie followed. As she passed him he caught her eye, touched a gentle hand to her elbow. "Did it go all right?"

His concern was for her. She didn't want to like him in this stupid, melting kind of way; she didn't want to be as aware of the simplest of touches as she was. She had to fight both those urges.

As if sensing something of her battle, Nick smiled, warmth in his eyes, and against her will she melted a little bit further. At that moment, Melody looked back over her shoulder, and just as quickly looked away again. But she had seen Nick's hand on her arm, his smile, and a small puzzled frown had drawn her brows together.

The family sat outside for dinner, grouped around a long, rustic dinning table. Candles on twisting, wax-covered, wrought-iron holders lined the center. A vine-covered pergola partially screened the dusky sky. Two men Callie recognized from Melody's bridal party joined them. Nick, who was seated opposite her, introduced them as his cousins, Michael, their head winemaker, who Callie had met earlier in the day, charming and urbane, and Ricardo, the vineyard manager, quiet, with what looked to be burn scars on the left side of his face.

And as for Nick's claim to have little to do with the winery and vineyard, it was obvious that the others had enormous respect for him, asking his opinion on matters both professional and personal.

Rosa supervised the bringing out of course after course, and dusk gave way to evening as the family ate and talked. Another cousin, Lisa, carrying a small baby girl, joined them partway through the meal, squeezing herself into a seat next to Nick. Callie had to make an effort not to stare in fascination at the baby cradled in its mother's arms. Sometimes it still didn't seem real that she, too, was going to be a mother.

She had anticipated the meal being strained. Nothing could have been further from reality. People talked over one another, argued and laughed. When Michael offered to pour Callie's wine and she declined, Melody sent her an odd glance. And twice Callie noticed Melody looking between her and Nick. But apart from the occasional searching glance, Nick paid her no special attention. He gave no hint that anything lay between them, showed no visible reaction when Michael flirted with her, though Callie knew he was aware of it. He joined in the conversation and was more relaxed than she'd seen him before. His dark eyes sparkled when he laughed. And he laughed often.

Callie felt included in a circle of warmth and friendship that she'd never experienced in her own family. It had the feeling of something deep and old and certain. Even when she had lived at home, she and her mother had seldom sat at the table. And there had definitely been none of this lingering and laughing and teasing.

She didn't want to like Nick, didn't want to see him as warm and caring, because it only highlighted what she couldn't have. And worse than that was the awful thought that this would be a wonderful environment for a child to grow up in. Much better than she, a single woman living on her own, could provide. This family, in itself, seemed *the village* that it supposedly took to raise a child.

As dessert was served, the baby became fractious and Lisa decided to leave. She passed the child to Nick so she could get out of her chair. Callie watched those big, competent hands take the baby, clearly comfortable with the infant. She saw the tears that had threatened vanish, to be replaced by a smile and then a small gurgling laugh.

Michael laughed and looked at Callie. "Nick's charm with the ladies is legendary." The hint of Italian in his accent was pronounced, because of the time he'd recently spent in Tuscany. "But you can see it is not ill-founded. It works even with babies."

Callie looked from Michael to the baby to Nick, confident and at ease.

And watching her.

His gaze challenged her, seeming to say that this would be them one day. The child he held would be their own. As she met and held his gaze in wordless communication, a sense of wonder and connection settled over her. How could the concept of raising their child together be so very foreign, and yet seem almost right at the same time?

Something changed in his gaze—emotion surfaced from the still, green depths, flickered and then was gone. Frowning, Nick turned and handed the baby up to its mother, releasing Callie from the enthrallment of that gaze. Lisa stood, jiggling the child as she made her goodbyes, and passed on and accepted last-minute messages from and to her absent husband. She turned to Melody as she tucked a shawl around the baby. "How's the nursery coming along?"

A collective sigh rose up from the men at the table, and Melody scowled theatrically at them before turning back to Lisa, her chin high. "Good."

"But…" Ricardo prompted.

"The paint color," several voices whined in unison.

"Philistines." Melody turned to Callie. "You'll help

me with the paint color, won't you? You have such a good eye for color. And an understanding of the importance of getting the right shade." She shot another glare around the unsympathetic table.

Callie remembered how long they'd taken over the brochures for Cypress Rise. But in the end they had something they were both thrilled with. "Of course. I'd love to."

But it was two days later before they had the chance. As the two women climbed the stairs after another leisurely and loud family dinner, Callie noted Mel's hand come to rest on her stomach. "Is everything all right?"

Melody smiled widely, her gaze softening. "Perfect."

"It's not too much for you? The festival and everything?"

"No. Today for a change, I have boundless energy. I think this evening I'll even get some more work done in the nursery."

"What do you need to do?" Callie had no idea about nurseries, or what sort of equipment and preparations she'd need for a baby. Helping Melody was a good pretext for getting her own thinking in order. She wanted to do things right, wanted to show Nick that she could.

"I've picked out the furniture, but I still need the curtains, and I can't do that till I've chosen the paint color. And I've seen some borders that I really like too." Melody talked nonstop about her plans as she led Callie up the stairs. They stepped into a bright, cozy room that would get lovely morning sun. No curtains hung at the wide windows that gave a view of dark silhouettes of rolling hills. An ornate wooden cot occupied one corner of the room.

"I've narrowed it down to a choice between those two

yellows." Melody pointed out two squares among the dozen rough-edged patches of color painted onto the cream walls. "Which do you prefer?"

Callie studied them for a moment. Her thoughts wandered. She didn't even know where she'd be living when her child was born, let alone know what color she was going to paint the nursery.

Her gaze caught Melody's and she pulled her attention back to the paint. "The one on the left, the more buttery one. It has a warmer feel."

Melody crossed to the wall and touched the paint. "I was leaning toward this one too." She was still facing the wall when she next spoke. "I'm sorry for what I thought about you and Jason." She turned quickly, pinned Callie with her gaze. "For doubting you and thinking you were trying to hang on to him."

Honey, you're welcome to him, would have been the wrong answer. "I guess the late-night phone calls could have looked a little odd."

"They weren't that late, and it's not like you hung up or anything when I answered. I just got insecure."

Callie shrugged. "You didn't need to. Jason really loves you."

Melody turned and looked out the window. "I do know that. I was tired and hormonal and feeling a bit vulnerable about the pregnancy and everything."

"For what it's worth, Jason's a good man. And he loves you in a way he never cared for me." And lately Callie had come to realize that she, too, was capable of much stronger feelings than the unthreatening comfort of those she'd had for Jason. Just how much stronger she didn't want to analyze.

"Having him seemed too good to be true." Melody

ran her fingers along the windowsill. "And I thought that, if it seemed that good, then I was probably missing something."

"Life kicked you in the teeth a few times?"

Melody laughed. "Once or twice. My own fault, usually. That's why I tend to be overcautious."

"It's not your fault if someone treats you badly."

The smile vanished from Melody's lips. "I guess not. But sometimes you also have to take responsibility for the situation you find yourself in. And if need be, do the right thing to get yourself out of it. I didn't always do that soon enough."

"You don't have to explain."

"But I do need to apologize. Especially if we're going to be seeing a lot more of you."

"I'll be gone in a few days."

"But you and Nick?"

"Nick and I?" Callie asked, unsure what Melody suspected.

"He's never brought a girlfriend here before. I thought it must be serious."

"I'm only here for the festival, because of Marc. He hasn't told you there's anything between us?"

"No. But he never tells anyone anything. We all figure it out by watching. I was wondering already, and then this morning, when he took you on the tour of the winery and vineyard himself, instead of letting Michael do it."

The supposedly quick tour that had stretched to three hours without either of them realizing the passing of the time, because Callie had had so many questions and they had been talking and laughing. She had forgotten everything but the pleasure of being with him.

"And he seems to care about you," Melody added. "He watches you with a different kind of look in his eyes."

Callie shook her head. "The only reason I'm here is because of the festival." And the child she was carrying, who would be a part of this family. Nick had said that much. So, although the demarcation lines were blurred, they were still there.

"You watch him too."

She'd tried to disguise the fascination he held for her, tried to stop the fanciful daydreams that sometimes caught her unawares. Obviously, she'd have to try harder. She shrugged. "He's not hard to look at. None of the Brunicadi men are."

"No. But Michael's even better-looking, and you don't watch him."

If she argued that particular assertion, it would work against her, so Callie said nothing. But while Michael might be technically more perfect, he didn't have the intensity that was so intriguing in Nick, didn't have the depths in his eyes.

"All the same. It's not what you're thinking."

"Oh. Sorry." Melody headed for the door. "I guess it's for the best. Nick's relationships never last long. He always ends them before they get serious."

Callie stifled a yawn as she held up a skirt and top. She met her gaze in the mirror and sternly repeated Melody's words: "His relationships never last long." She'd do well to heed that warning, a repetition of what she already knew, but was in danger of dismissing.

Keep her mind on the job, that was all she had to do, not on thoughts of Nick, on his rare smile, on the hidden depths in his eyes.

She could want far more than she should from the Nick she'd come to know. Far more than he would be prepared to give.

The festival was the day after tomorrow. And the day after that she would be leaving. She only had to shore up her battered defenses for that long.

She was a professional. She could do it.

She surveyed her reflection. The skirt and blouse would be good for tomorrow, but—she lifted her hand to her scalp—she really needed to wash her hair. *Soon,* she thought as she laid the clothes on her bed. She'd wash her hair soon. She'd managed it one-handed a couple of times. It was awkward and tiring, but not impossible.

In the living room she sat on the couch and opened her laptop. But instead of rechecking the schedule for tomorrow as she'd intended, she called up one of the Internet sites she'd found on pregnancy, looked at the image of a fetus cocooned in a womb and tried to concentrate on the information swimming in front of her. Leaning back, she closed her eyes.

"Callie." The softly spoken word, the hand on her shoulder, startled her.

She spun to see Nick beside her on the couch. "Where did you come from?"

His eyes were narrowed with concern. "I knocked."

"I must have dozed off."

"You think?" His face softened, humor lit his eyes.

"It's been a long day."

The amusement vanished. "That's why I wanted to check on you. You looked a little tired at dinner and my family doesn't exactly let a person get a word in edgewise. From my office, I can see some of the comings and goings at the winery. You didn't stop all day. And then Melody dragged you up to the nursery. You need to take it easier. Learn to say no."

"Nick, I'm fine." He'd been watching her? Even as she thought about him and wondered where he was and what he was doing?

"So fine that you're falling asleep while you're still trying to work." He gestured to her laptop on the coffee table, the screen saver meandering across the screen. "Go to bed, Callie," he said gently.

"I will. As soon as I wash my hair." She speared her fingers through her curls. "And actually," she admitted, "I wasn't working. I meant to, but…" She leaned forward to touch the mouse pad and the screen came to life in front of them. The picture of the baby was still there.

Nick was quiet for a moment. "I've been looking at these sites, as well. There's so much to learn."

"I know." She kept her gaze trained on the screen, focused her thoughts on the image there. And not on the man sitting a whisper away from her. "Sometimes I can hardly believe it's all real. That it's happening to me. Maybe once I feel her kicking. But they say—" she scrolled down a couple of pages "—that that won't happen till around sixteen weeks."

In wordless agreement, they looked through the sites each of them had found, exclaiming, and a little awestruck at what was happening. Callie only wished she wasn't equally captivated by Nick's hands on the keyboard, the dexterous fingers, the tanned forearms exposed by the rolled-up sleeves of his shirt. And if only she was as good as Nick at ignoring their inadvertent touches—a brush of shoulder or knee. The touches that sent heat coiling through her.

If they didn't have a guaranteed future together that

needed to be negotiated, she could want so much from this man. *For now,* she told herself. *Only for now.*

As he navigated the sites she stole glances at his profile, the faint shadow of beard on his jaw, the seriousness of his expression. She liked, a little too much, that he'd been doing his own research.

He turned, caught her watching him. She looked quickly back at the screen.

"What's it like? For you." His voice was quiet, earnest.

She met the gaze that was now intent on her. It was several seconds before she could gather her thoughts to answer. "It's like…magic. I can't believe it's real. And yet it is." She placed her hand over her stomach. "And I guess it's kind of scary too. There's so much I don't know."

"Are you worried about the birth, about the hospital?"

"No. Not yet."

"But you will be?"

"Probably."

"I'll be there." His eyes scanned her face.

"You will be?"

"Yes." There was no hesitation in his response, and still that green gaze was trained on her. Waiting.

"But do *you* want me there?"

Callie turned back to the computer screen. "Yes." She couldn't think of anyone she'd rather have there than Nick, with his quiet strength. She just didn't want him to see quite how much she wanted it.

They looked at a few more sites, but when Callie stifled a yawn Nick stood.

"You need to go to bed. Now."

Callie stood too. "As soon as I've washed my hair."

"I'll help you."

"It's okay. I'll manage."

"I'll help you." He strode to the bathroom, and soon the sound of the shower running reached her.

Callie followed him. Steam billowed from the shower and splashes of water dampened his pale shirt.

"You wet it. I'll do the shampoo."

"Nick."

"What?" he asked, as though he really couldn't see why she'd have a problem with him washing her hair. And maybe he was right. She was pregnant with his child. Having his hands in her hair could do no further harm.

"Nothing. Just turn away for a second, would you?"

He turned his back. "I have seen you naked before."

Callie ignored his words as she peeled off her clothes and stepped into the shower, grateful that, from knee to chin height, the glass was smoky and opaque. "This is different."

He turned back and leaned against the far wall, arms folded across his chest as she sluiced water over her hair. "Pass me a towel please?" she asked once it was thoroughly wet.

Nick held one of the thick, cream towels out to her. Callie shut off the water and reached a hand through the door, took the towel and wrapped it around herself before stepping out of the shower. She pushed her shampoo bottle into his hand, folded her arms across her chest, anchoring the towel under her armpits, and closed her eyes.

And waited.

She opened one eye. Nick stood close. He wasn't smiling, but she could see the dimple in his left cheek as he studied her.

"It's not going to hurt."

She closed her eye again. "Just get on with it, would you," she snapped.

And now she was sure he was smiling. Her own lips twitched. And then those strong, capable hands were on her head, massaging shampoo through her hair. And suddenly there was nothing remotely funny about her situation. He surrounded her, his arms either side of her face. And if she opened her eyes, she'd see his chest inches in front of her. She closed her eyes tighter. Beneath the fragrance of her shampoo she caught the faintest trace of his cologne.

"Rinse." He turned her back to face the shower.

Callie dropped the towel and stepped in.

Please let him not know how hard her heart was pounding when, a few minutes later, she reached a second time for the towel and passed him her conditioner. His hands were slower this time, fingertips sliding across her scalp. The strength threatened to flee from her knees. His hands moved to the back of her head, massaging, the pressure of his touch exquisite. Callie kept her eyes closed as a desire that she couldn't let him see built low within her. Her breath grew shallower, and suddenly his hands paused as they cupped her head.

Her eyes flew open in time to see him hesitate before he lowered his head. And then he was kissing her, his mouth hard and hungry. And she was most definitely kissing him back. Greedily. Her towel forgotten, her arms slid around him, even as a part of her brain whispered feebly, *don't do this.* That part of her brain was effortlessly overpowered and ignored by the demands of her body. The need for his touch, for this closeness. It was everything she feared because it was everything she wanted.

Strong hands held her head as he deepened the kiss. His tongue swept her mouth, learning anew her taste.

Joining them. In primal response, she pressed her hips into his and felt the evidence of his need. His hands slid over dampened skin to grip her shoulders. He kissed her jaw, her neck, inflaming her. He was all she remembered. And more. Being with him, she could forget everything.

Just as she had that night.

That night that had gotten her pregnant.

Callie broke the kiss. "Nick," she gasped his name, shaking her head. "No." She wanted him fiercely, desperately, but also she wanted more than just this.

He stepped back, regret etched into his face. "Rinse." He turned and left.

Nick came out of the winery building, where he'd been talking with Michael about this year's vintage and the likely effect of the summer's weather patterns. With only one day till the festival, the grounds were alive with hurrying people and shouted communications, as marquees were set up, tables and chairs delivered and a myriad of other jobs commenced or finished. He scanned the activity, found what he sought as he caught sight of Callie in a summery skirt and sleeveless blouse, looking as fresh as new leaves on the vines in springtime.

She'd kept her distance from him today. Undoubtedly a good thing. She had sensed the driving need that had slammed into him last night. He had wanted her. Wanted to back her up against the bathroom cabinet and claim her.

But she wasn't his.

She had her own life, her own dreams. Dreams of love and happy families. She'd told him that when she'd explained why she wouldn't want to marry him.

And he had his life too.

If only he could stop the desire that ambushed him every time he saw her.

They shared a baby; and because of that child they had to have a relationship that worked and that lasted. Sex, as desperately tempting as it was, would only confuse matters and quite probably destroy that something else, that tentative bond—the one that should terrify him but didn't—that was building between them.

He liked knowing she was near, it had a sense of rightness. And at mealtimes, when everyone gathered around the outdoor table, she blended in—a natural part, giving as good as she got from his cousins. His family liked her.

And she liked them.

An idea was beginning to percolate, a plan that capitalized on her emotions and that would meet both of their needs. He would tell her tomorrow, after the festival.

She looked his way, then quickly looked away again. She was in professional mode, elegant, efficient, but a little repressed. Her secrets and dreams hidden. And she was still working too hard, accepting the demands placed on her from all directions.

He wanted to take her away from all this, he wanted to make her laugh, he wanted to see her again in that enormous paint-splattered shirt. That was the Callie who fascinated him; that was the Callie who for one night had danced in his arms and who had trusted herself. And him.

And look where that had got them.

She stood talking to Noah, the glass artist whose blue heron in flight hung suspended in a window alcove of the winery's reception area. An artist, just as she was at heart. Did his devil-may-care appearance, his carved jade necklace, appeal to her? It was hard to tell from this distance whether or not Noah was standing too close. Callie pointed to her left, describing something with her hands.

Nick would make her his. He didn't want anyone else to know the scent of her hair. *He* knew it. It had enveloped him in the steamy bathroom. It had lingered on his fingers through the night. And he would never catch that scent again without thinking of her. The sun shone on her dark curls now. They would capture and hold that heat. If he plunged his fingers—

Snap out of it.

The turning away got harder each time, but he managed it again. It would be too easy to be swept up in her. To think of nothing and no one else. The battle within was constant.

His previous relationships had been easy, possibly superficial. That was how he liked them. There was nothing easy about what he felt for Callie. He'd seen the mirror of wanting in her eyes. But she was the one who'd had the strength to end their kiss. She was looking for happiness, for forever. He couldn't give her those things, but he could and would provide for and protect her.

One of the catering staff hurried out of a marquee, heading for Callie. Nick strode to intercept him. The least he could do was lighten a workload that she would deny needed lightening.

Ten

Callie surveyed the crowd of festival goers, almost ready to breathe a sigh of relief. The morning had opened with a line of people waiting at the gates, and had got steadily busier. The weather was being kind, a gentle breeze taking the edge off the oppressive heat. Still, nearly all the guests wore sun hats and made the most of the shade covers and marquees set up around the public areas. The headline jazz band had started up, and beneath the sultry strains of the saxophone came the sounds of laughter, conversation and the clink of glasses. So far, so good. To the casual observer, the day was running with effortless efficiency.

"Ms. Jamieson." Robert, a young vineyard worker, appeared in front of Callie, his breathing heavy.

She nodded for him to continue. What new crisis, imagined or real, needed to be dealt with? Efficiency was never effortless.

"There's a problem with the sculpture of the jazz trio. Something to do with the bass player."

Callie sighed and started walking between two rows of vines, heading for the gleaming stainless-steel assemblage of nuts and bolts and old machinery parts that comprised the strangely animated sculpture. She only had to hang in there for a few more hours. Then the guests would be gone, and the cleanup and moving crews could start. And then she could take a break.

Nick had found her an hour ago and suggested she take a break then. He didn't understand that she needed to be on hand to deal with issues just like this one. His eyes had told her he thought she was making excuses. He also didn't seem to understand that she needed to be busy—so she didn't think about him, that kiss, the way she wanted him to hold her. So yes, maybe it had been partly an excuse.

As she passed the end of a row, a hand snaked out and grasped her wrist, tugging her off balance and against a warm, hard body.

Callie recognized his scent and the solid feel of Nick behind her. Her back pressed into his broad chest. His fingers encircled her wrists. And for a second she stood there letting him support her, cradle her, letting his strength seep into her. She allowed herself the brief luxury, then tried to pull away. "I need to get to The Jazz Players."

He held firm to her wrists and she felt the movement of him shaking his head behind her. "There's nothing wrong with The Jazz Players." His deep voice was warm in her ear.

"Robert just told me there was a problem."

Nick's hands skimmed up her bare arms, his touch like the dance of a firefly. His hands rested on her shoulders and he turned her to face him, to put a little more distance between them. Not nearly enough for her comfort. "The only problem is you not taking a break all day long. You brushed me off when I suggested it earlier. Now I'm making it happen. I know the perfect spot."

She studied his face, the deep green of his eyes. She should argue, but some time alone with Nick—in the safety of daylight—tempted her powerfully. She nodded. She was leaving tomorrow, she would take what moments she could.

The handheld radio buzzed at her waist. She reached for it, but Nick was quicker, whisking it out of her reach and turning it off. "It's nothing that can't wait."

"But—"

He sighed and grasped her hand, his touch warm and sure. "There are plenty of people here to help out. They'll deal with whatever it is." He tugged her up a gentle slope, away from the jazz and the art and the crowds, to a secluded spot on a hill beneath a spreading oak tree. A picnic rug lay on the ground, a wicker basket resting in its center, a golden baguette poking temptingly out from beneath the lid.

"Sit."

He'd done this. For her? Callie lowered herself down gratefully.

"A glass of water? Or would you prefer something stronger? I've packed soda and orange juice."

Callie smiled. "Water, thanks." She watched his hands and the play of muscle in his forearms as he unscrewed the cap from a bottle of mineral water and poured the liquid into two elegant wineglasses. "You don't have to drink water just because I am." He didn't answer, just passed a glass to her and raised his own in a silent toast. Callie took a sip.

Nick started pulling food from the basket. "I've discovered that pregnant woman are exceedingly difficult to pack a picnic for. Apparently, you're supposed to be wary of cold meats, and soft cheeses and pâtés."

"Everything that makes for a good picnic." She tried not to let it show how touched she was that he'd taken the trouble to find out what she should and shouldn't eat. He was just being Nick. Whatever he did, he did well.

"Not everything." He sliced the baguette into chunks, and his heavy silver watch glinted in the sun as he produced an array of plastic tubs containing everything from butter and mayonnaise to cheddar cheese and artichoke hearts—and of course grapes, as well as pineapple and mangoes. She couldn't stop the strange softening within her.

"What about Melody?"

"Melody has other family looking out for her." Nick filled a plate with food. "It's you I'm concerned about. Now eat," he said, as he passed her the plate. Callie suddenly discovered she was not only tired but ravenous, and a picnic lunch seemed like the best idea in the world. Nick filled his own plate, and they ate to the distant strains of jazz drifting through the vines.

"How did you know this is exactly what I needed?" she asked a little later as she bit into a strawberry, the last thing on her plate.

Nick watched as, with her other hand, she brushed crumbs from her front. "It was fairly obvious."

Callie lay back on the blanket and watched the sky through the filter of the leaves above her. She closed her eyes, resting her hands on her stomach. Nick stretched out beside her.

The silence lengthened, and the awareness that he

was watching her grew. She chanced a glance at him from beneath her lashes, saw his eyes fixed not on her face but on her abdomen. His gaze flicked upward and caught her scrutiny. She saw a movement, felt his touch as he picked her hand up and shifted it to rest on her ribs. His palm, broad and flat, settled over her stomach. Just that. No more. He held it there absolutely still. Her thoughts went to the child inside her, her first hello from her father. Ever since Rosa's pronouncement, she'd thought of the baby as a girl. A three-way connection, baby and both its parents.

It felt so very right.

She remembered how, back in her hotel room, Nick had also said the baby was a girl. "The other night, why did you say the baby was a girl?"

His fingers spanned wider across her abdomen. "Did I say that?"

"Yes. Just like Rosa did."

"Huh." The sound was noncommittal and vaguely disbelieving. "There's a fifty-fifty chance."

"You sounded certain."

His hand shifted, picked up hers and placed it back where his had rested. She missed the gentle weight of his touch.

"No. How could I be?" His fingers skimmed up and back down her arm, trailing warmth.

"Are you like Rosa? Do you know things?"

The hand stilled. "No."

"I've heard that in the financial markets they call you The Profit, but that it's a play on words. That you do seem to be unusually lucky."

"People like to call skill and hard work 'luck.' It makes them feel better. I've had my share of losses too.

They forget about those when it suits them. And Rosa, she gets lucky sometimes, but she's wrong sometimes too. I wouldn't paint the nursery pink on her say-so."

"Melody thinks Rosa's right about her baby being a boy."

"Like I say, there's a fifty-fifty chance she is right. Melody's happy to buy into it."

Callie was silent for a while. "Do you remember the painting at my home? The one you said reminded you of Cathedral Cove?"

"Yes." There was hesitation in the way he drew out the word.

"I painted it there."

He paused a beat. "You did a good job. You have talent."

"It was only the water. No landmarks, not the hole in the rocks."

"The water there has a certain quality, don't you think? It must have, otherwise you wouldn't have painted it."

"Maybe." It was her turn to be noncommittal. His refusal to share that something of himself she sensed, hurt.

As she studied him she was hit with a knowledge herself. She could want this man. No. Not could. Did. Certainly, she wanted more of him than he was willing to give. She knew his touch, his kiss, and wanted it again. It was dangerous territory to let her thoughts wander to. "The turnout is fantastic."

"Mmm."

"Right in line with our most optimistic predictions."
Come on, Nick, help me out. Give me something to stop me thinking about the shadow of beard on your jaw.

"Mmm."

Stop me thinking about lacing my fingers between

yours. "If gate sales keep up at the rate they have been we may have to restrict numbers."

"Callie."

"Yes."

"I brought you here to have a break."

She lapsed into silence, but unable to stop looking, she continued to study Nick, stretched out on his back, hands clasped behind his head, biceps curving against the sleeves of his polo shirt. A smudge of grease streaked above his elbow. His eyes were closed and his dark lashes rested lightly on tanned cheeks. It would be too easy to just lie there drinking in details of his appearance.

"Close your eyes."

How did he know? Quickly, she shut her eyes and tried to relax; but lying so close to him made her too conscious of his nearness. Awareness vibrated through her. If she didn't talk business she'd think about him, maybe do something stupid like reach out and touch him. "Almost half the artwork has sold already."

He expelled a sigh of exasperation.

Callie pushed on, warming to the topic. "And I think there's someone interested in the copper dragon. That's our most expensive piece."

He gave a sudden low growl and she heard the rustle of movement. The light that had dappled her face gave way to shadow. She opened her eyes. Nick loomed over her. For a second their gazes locked. Then with another softer, shorter growl, he lowered his head and his lips claimed hers.

Callie's mouth parted beneath his. He tasted of sunshine—heat and light. Sensation bloomed and overwhelmed her. Her hands went to his shoulders, the muscles hard and contoured beneath her touch. Kissing him was like stepping into a fantasy. Her senses swam. Reality threatened to slip away beneath the magic of his touch. His fingers slid up her jawline, threading into her hair, cupping her head, drawing her closer yet for the demands of his mouth.

Her hands found their way to the dark warmth of his hair, the strong column of his neck, the silken steel of his shoulders. He held her to him, his body pressed along the length of hers. Against her will, forgetting all the reasons she shouldn't be doing this, she arched into him, pressed her hips to his, driven by a compulsion to get closer still. A hint of beard gently abraded the sensitized skin of her jaw. His hand cupped her breast through the fabric of her blouse. Just that, an exquisite, almost unbearable touch, and a small moan of pleasure escaped her.

"Callie."

She loved the sound of her name on his lips. "Yes."

"A bed."

"Yes." The single syllable was all she was capable of. It threatened to turn into a mantra and a plea.

In the privacy of the guest cottage, the strong hands she loved to look at, loved the feel of, slid up her arms, over the curve of her shoulders till they cupped her face. Long fingers slid into her hair as he lowered his head.

He kissed her for the longest time. Holding her close against the masculine warmth and solidity of his body, savoring her. And greedily she drank in the taste and feel of him, clung to the power and vitality of him.

Standing here, kissing this man, Callie felt more at one with him than she'd ever felt with another human. She carried his child. She knew him. He knew and understood her. She'd never had that before.

The ceiling fan spun lazily above them as his mouth moved over hers, and they made their way slowly across the room till the bed pressed against the backs of her legs. And still they kissed. His lips explored and pleasured. He savored her like he savored a fine wine. Sipping gently, searching for every nuance with tongue and lips and seeking hands.

Those hands shifted, found the hem of her blouse, slid underneath till warm palms skimmed over the sensitized skin, trailing fire in their wake. His fingers traced the contours of her body as his tongue learned her mouth with slow, sweet seduction. Palms cupped the weight of her breasts, his thumbs grazed over lace-covered nipples, spearing need through her.

She had wanted to give, but that wanting threatened to be overpowered by the consuming need to take. Nick lifted his head and studied her. She saw the need and desire in his darkened eyes. He reached again for her. Slowly, he slipped each of her buttons undone till he could brush apart the sides of her blouse. Lowering his head, he closed his mouth over the thin lace, dampening the fabric and the tight aching nipple beneath it. Compulsion arched her against him, into him, her hands slid through the dark, sun-warmed silk of his hair, pulling his head closer yet.

His fingers slipped under the thin lace strap on her shoulder, grazed it across and down her arm. He lifted his mouth only long enough to ease the fabric aside and expose already dampened flesh to the air before his mouth again closed over her, hot and seeking. The faint stubble of his jaw grazed her flushed skin. His tongue flicked and her body jerked in reflex as a desperate gasp escaped her.

Reaching for his shirt, she sought access to the warmth of his smooth skin and the muscles beneath. Layer by layer, seeking hands knocking and tangling, they peeled away each other's clothes—her blouse, his shirt, her skirt, his pants—until there were no barriers between them.

The stillness of awe and wonder settled over her at the sheer male beauty of him. Stark planes and contours. Like a creature of a fantasy world. Her fantasy world.

And in return, the heat of his gaze, the hunger and raw need in his eyes swept through her, inflamed her. "Calypso." Her name was husky, strangled, on his lips. And that one simple word, spoken that way by him, threatened to buckle her knees.

Then he was moving, touching her again, guiding her till they lay down together on the softness of his bed. They touched. Fingertips to skin, lips to lips. The touch grew fevered as desire burned brighter. She hadn't known wanting the like of it before. This fierce desperation. She wanted to take and she wanted to give. But she needed this moment too. The exploration, the appreciation, the slowness, gentleness and oneness.

Her palm grazed over a small, hardened nipple, settled over the strong beat of his heart. And in her mind she claimed his heart with that gesture. Claimed it for herself. For always.

He groaned, and she reveled in the contradictions of that sound, powerlessness and fierceness in one. An echo of her own paradox. How was it possible to feel the strength of a warrior and utter languidness at the same time? To be flying and falling? Demanding and surrendering?

She was his if he only knew it. This man who cared so deeply, loved so thoroughly.

She'd known his body before and yet everything was different, everything had changed between them. Sensation dizzied her, carried her like Dorothy's tornado out of a world she knew and into a realm more vivid than she could have imagined.

Her skin was alive to his touch. In the warm glow of sunlight her eyes saw only him, the half-lowered eyelids, the line of his jaw, the curve of his throat and shoulder. Her hands felt only him, curving muscle, heated silken skin.

Desire grew fiercer, exquisitely unbearable till it became a clawing, clamoring need, overpowering everything.

He raised himself over her and she opened to him, guided him into her. She met him, clung to him. Her hands slid from shoulders, to hips, to taut muscle, needing him closer yet.

With a ripple of powerful hips he thrust deeper, and she rose to meet him so that he filled her completely.

He bent his head and kissed her. So gentle, so fiercely erotic.

The moved together, two bodies with one entwining purpose. Slowly. Exquisitely. And then inexorably faster, desire flaming and obliterating restraint or even thought until only dizzying sensations and desperate need remained. And love.

She called his name as release pulsed through them.

The laughter and the camaraderie of dinner washed around and over Callie, and filled her with an aching sense of loneliness. She couldn't let herself be seduced by this world. A world she couldn't have. A world she almost desperately wished she belonged to. This was the family life she imagined when she allowed herself to dream.

The prospect of going home tomorrow and carrying on with her life felt unbelievably hollow.

She should be happy. The festival had been an un-qualified success, and that was what she'd come here for. Nothing more. The money that would now go to the teenage shelter was at the top end of their most optimistic predictions. A good thing. Professionally.

Personally, she was a mess.

She had made love with Nick. Worse than that, she *loved* Nick. And she had no idea how he felt.

She would be flying out of Sydney tomorrow. And she didn't want to go. So much had changed. For the short time she'd been here she'd been happy. And the biggest part of that happiness had been Nick. Knowing he was there for support, for help, to talk with, to laugh with, to sit quietly with in the evening. Part of her was conscious of his whereabouts if he was near, and alert for his return if he wasn't. Things felt right this way. Yet it wasn't going to be.

He didn't do commitment.

She, however, did, and her commitment at the moment had to be to her business—her clients and staff back home. And in looking after them, she would be providing a future for herself and her child.

The family was lingering over coffee when she looked up to find Nick watching her. He stood, came around to Callie and held a hand out for her. "Come with me, there's something I want to show you."

With just that gesture and those words she suddenly felt that everything would be all right.

Half a dozen pairs of curious eyes followed them as they left. She sat with him in the Range Rover as he drove a few miles down the road, pointing out places of interest, pointing out other vineyards. He was Nick the tour guide. It was as though their lovemaking had never happened. He took a turn onto a smaller road, following it as it wound up into the hills.

After several minutes driving, they rounded a corner and he pulled over on the crest of a hill almost facing back the way they had come. The valley spread out below them, bathed in the golden glow of the sunset.

"What do you think?"

"It's beautiful. I've always loved the light and shadows of sunset. Look at the way the clouds are lit up." So beautiful it made her ache. Like being with him made her ache.

He smiled and that ache deepened. "So, you like it here?"

There was so much she liked here. The place cast a spell over her that was an extension of the one the man himself seemed to cast. Something about it, about him, threatened to make her forget herself. "What's not to like? The valley, the hills."

He pulled back. "Not the view, which I'll admit is beautiful, but the bungalow."

She followed the direction of his gaze. A little way ahead and to their right, partially screened by tall poplars, stood a spreading white bungalow, encircled by a deep wisteria-covered veranda. Callie could picture an easel set up on the veranda, imagine herself painting the valley through the seasons and the changing of the light.

She looked back at Nick. "It's gorgeous."

"It's one of ours. Lisa lived here when she first came to work for us a year ago as a lab technician. Then she met and married Gregory."

"She seems like she's been part of your family for years."

"She fitted in from the very start. You do too," he added quietly.

"They're easy to be with."

"They can be overwhelming. Lisa maintained that this place—" he pointed to the bungalow "—was the perfect distance. Close to the family and the winery. But not too close. It gets good light too. For your painting."

Callie watched him, uncertain. "Could we back this conversation up a little? Why would I be painting here?"

"Not just painting. Living."

A flare of hope ignited within her. She didn't dare trust it. "You're suggesting what?"

"That you move here."

Just that? That she uproot her life and shift here. She waited, but he added nothing further. The hope withered. It took several seconds before she found her voice. "I'm not going to live here. I have a home back in New Zealand. A business. Clients."

"You can work from here, or Sydney if you need to. The flights back to New Zealand are quick and regular. And you said yourself that your lease on your place is about to expire. Think about it." His voice was calm, patient. "You like it here. You've said as much."

He'd thought about everything. Made it sound so rational. But there had been no mention of those things that weren't rational, like feelings, like love. Nick the tour guide was suggesting she move here, not Nick the lover. The man she wanted to…love.

"And of course, you're having my baby."

She laid a protective hand over her stomach. "That's not the issue."

His gaze followed the movement, then he looked back up at her. "It's very much the issue. It's the beginning and end of the issue."

Meaning, if there was no baby he wouldn't care where she lived. Her head was spinning. "You're serious, aren't you? You actually think I'm going to move to the Hunter Valley to suit your convenience." The sad thing was that a part of her, the vulnerable part, desperately wanted to at least consider it.

"Think about it, Callie. It could work. We like each other well enough. I'd be able to see you and our baby regularly."

"You like me well enough." She couldn't keep the incredulity from her voice. She'd thought she hadn't needed Melody's warning, thought she was in no danger from Nick. But the danger had crept up nonetheless. And she was vulnerable to him. More than vulnerable, she realized. She'd gone right ahead and fallen in love with him. A man who didn't have the word *love* in his vocabulary. Not the type of love she wanted to give him and to have from him. She felt like she was about to crumple in on the sudden emptiness within herself.

"So, let me get this straight." She kept her voice level, didn't want to betray the fragility of her emotions. "Because I'm having your child, and there's a house free on one of your vineyards, and because it would be convenient for you, and we 'like' each other well enough— I should uproot my life and come and live here? For what, Nick?"

Nick didn't say anything.

"What about sex? You forgot that. Maybe you could come over sometimes for sex too. I mean, we know that's good between us."

"You're taking this all wrong. Getting worked up about something simple. I'm trying to make this easy for you."

"You're trying to make it easy for yourself. You get all the benefits without having to make any changes. Without even having to open your heart a little."

His gaze narrowed. "You refused marriage." Finally that reasonable tone cracked and exasperation crept in. "This is the perfect compromise, a stepping stone."

She had no response.

"What do you want from me?"

That was the crux of the matter. She looked out her window. She couldn't say "love." It wouldn't be fair to him, when, at least in that regard, he'd been honest. She was like all those other foolish, blind women who'd fallen for him. But what about the possibility of it? "Nothing," she said slowly. "I don't want anything from you."

"This is the obvious solution." He tried again. Reasonable, logical, as though he hadn't heard her. "It could work really well for us all."

She shook her head. "This is so not the obvious solution. I have a business to run and it's based in New Zealand." It was Ivy Cottage that gave her independence. She was thinking, belatedly, of protecting her heart. And for that she needed to be away from this man who was offering her nothing of himself.

"You wouldn't even have to keep working, unless you wanted to." He countered. "I'm happy to support you for as long as you want. You could sell Ivy Cottage to Marc, I'll finance him."

He'd tried to think of everything, but he'd missed the one thing she wanted most of all, the one thing he couldn't or wouldn't give: something of himself. "You have all the answers, don't you."

"I'm trying to be logical."

"It can't always be about logic."

"What is it about, then?" His gaze searched her face. She didn't answer, couldn't tell him.

"All right then, put it this way, I'm trying to do the right thing. I thought we were both going to try to do what was best for the baby."

"Best for the baby or best for you?" she snapped. "What about this 'obvious' solution? I can find a place for *you* to move to, near where *I* live."

"Whoa." He held up his hands in a gesture of surrender. "How about we forget I said anything?"

But he said it, not in a *maybe I was wrong and I'm sorry* kind of voice, but in an *obviously you're not rational at the moment and you need to calm down* voice.

"Gladly." But what she wouldn't forget was that all his reasons had been practical. An ache swelled in her heart. There had been no mention of him feeling anything at all for her beyond the pale *like*. He would fit her into a corner of his life, and she was supposed to be content with that, be grateful for the crumbs he offered her.

It wasn't going to happen. She closed her eyes and made that promise to herself. She'd compromised before and she wouldn't do it again. Not when she was the only one doing the compromising.

Nick started the Range Rover, pulled slowly back out into the road, swinging around to head back the way they had come.

They drove in cold silence. He stopped at the guest cottage. Neither of them spoke as she got out.

Eleven

Callie sat in the Range Rover, Melody at her side driving. "I appreciate you taking me back to Sydney." The lump was still there in her throat, where it had lodged last night, a smaller version of the one in her chest.

"It works out really well." Melody smiled, oblivious. "I want to see my obstetrician anyway. I've been getting some odd twinges. I'll stay at Nick's apartment tonight and meet Jason off the plane tomorrow. Then we're going to go and look at nursery furniture."

Callie felt a pang of envy. Shopping for nursery furniture with the father of her baby was not going to happen for her.

"Besides, it's the least I could do, after all the work you did for the festival. It felt so good to be able to help out the shelter, and as a bonus, the vineyard's profile has gone right up. The publicity you got for us was fantastic." Melody started talking about the vineyard and her plans for it. Callie tried to keep up. Tried to stop her thoughts going back to last night.

She had dreaded going down to breakfast almost as much as she had wanted to see Nick. The dread and the wanting were wasted. He hadn't been there. That was enough of a signal that he didn't care about what she said. The loss threatened to swamp her.

She had to take just one day at a time. Today was the day to go home and regroup, to figure out what was happening to her, which of her feelings were real and which were a by-product of the situation she was in and of capricious pregnancy hormones. Because she knew one thing for certain—her feelings for Nick were completely out of the realm of her experience. She knew now the love that could be so much more than the pale imitation she'd had before. But the pain increased in proportion.

Focus on the here and now. That was all she could do.

"Are you still expecting me to believe there's nothing between you and Nick?"

Callie glanced at Melody. If anything, there was even less between them than when Melody had last asked. "Nick and I have some things to sort out," Callie conceded. "But it's not what you're thinking."

"I was thinking you're pregnant."

Callie stiffened. "Why do you say that?" Was the whole family psychic?

"You haven't drunk any wine the whole time you've been here. And the only other person doing that is me. Rosa's knitting a pink cardigan, which I know isn't for Junior. And sometimes you touch your stomach and look the way I feel. Awed."

Melody's reasons at least were sound. Callie took a deep breath and answered. "Yes."

"And Nick's the father."

Not a question. A statement.

"Yes."

"So, what—"

"It's complicated." And it wasn't anything she felt like talking about.

For a moment, Mel's expression didn't change, and then a delighted smile lit her face. "I don't care what you say. That's wonderful."

Obviously, to her the complications meant nothing. Callie, on the other hand, had to fight the threat of another wave of tears.

"When are you due?"

At least that was a question she could answer. "Mid-September."

"Two months after me. Junior will have a cousin almost the same age."

This so wasn't where Callie wanted to go, talking of the future and family relationships. But she needn't have worried. Melody wasn't looking for any answers from her. "Have you had morning sickness? Mine was awful at first. Not just mornings, but all day long."

They drove, Melody's conversation darting from pregnancy symptoms to birthing options, and the best stores to buy nursery equipment. Callie got the feeling Melody probably even had plans for where her child would go to college. She envied her that certainty.

Melody's hand dropped to her abdomen, pressed against it, and for an instant her mouth tightened. "Nick's a good man." Another sudden conversational switch.

"I know. But his relationships never last." Melody's own words.

She was silent for several seconds. "I know I said that. And it's true. But they haven't lasted before because he hasn't wanted them to. He doesn't let people get close. Sometimes he'll even push them away. Deliberately distance himself."

Wasn't that the truth?

Melody patted her stomach, but her palm closed into a fist against it and she winced.

"Are you all right?"

"It was a cramp. I've had a few today. I don't know what they are. It's too early for Braxton Hicks contractions." The color had drained from her face.

"Shall I drive?" Callie offered.

"That might be a good idea. I'm sure I'm fine. The first trimester is the riskiest period, and I'm into my second now. But I am a little tired."

Melody guided the car to the shoulder of the road and they swapped places. Once in the passenger seat, Melody reclined it and closed her eyes, but a frown pleated her brow and she kept her hands clasped over her abdomen. Concern tightened Callie's grip on the wheel, and she drove as fast as she legally and safely could.

As they came into the city, Melody directed Callie to her obstetrician's offices. By now, Mel was white and tears were swimming in her eyes.

Callie went around to her side of the car and opened the door. Mel got out and doubled over. That was when Callie saw the blood.

Callie was sitting at the side of Mel's hospital bed, holding her hand, when the door swung open. Nick strode into the room and halted. His gaze darted between them, fear and questions in his eyes, then settled on Melody. "How are you?" His voice gentle, hurting.

Mel opened her mouth to speak but no words came out, instead her tears started all over again. Callie didn't feel that she had the right to hers, but they fell anyway, as they had throughout the afternoon, for Mel, for Jason, for the baby who would never be.

Nick crossed slowly to his sister, hugged her. Melody's arms snaked around his shoulders, and she clung to him, still crying. Feeling like she was intruding, Callie stood to go. Nick looked at her and mouthed the word, *stay*.

Her heart breaking a hundred different ways, Callie shook her head and left. Nothing had changed for them.

Nick leaned against a corner post of the veranda, his fists in his pockets in a parody of nonchalance that he was light years from feeling. When Callie had turned and walked away a week ago, he'd told himself that he could let her go. That through grim determination, he could make himself not need her. But even before she'd gone from his sight, he knew with blinding clarity that wasn't ever going to happen. He no longer wanted to live the shutdown existence of his past. He would do whatever he had to to get her back into his life.

Permanently.

Melody had lost her baby. He was not going to lose Callie or their child. Because he—who hadn't thought he needed anyone—needed Calypso Jamieson with every breath he took. He needed her spirit and her laughter. And her love. In denying that, in letting her go, he'd made a colossal mistake. But now he was back to fix it.

It had taken all of the intervening days to set his plans in motion. And each and every one of those hollow days that had dragged by had only reinforced how vital she was to his existence.

He watched now as barefoot, she stepped through the open French doors of her villa. The first rays of sunlight caught her pale face and she stilled. Her gaze swung unerringly toward him, her brown eyes wide.

Like a thirsting man, he drank in the sight of her, and for long seconds the world stopped.

He shouldered off from the post and she looked away, breaking their tenuous contact, and glanced instead at the bright yellow mug cradled in her hands. Lifting her chin, she walked to the edge of the veranda. She set her mug down carefully and looked out over the rolling green countryside. White-knuckled fingers gripped the railing.

He studied her profile, her dark curls loose about her face, as she stood there aloof and alone as he'd seen her once before. Her oversize shirt, smudged in black and fresh, bloodred paint shrouded her body.

He took a step closer. "Is this loneliness or solitude?" His future hinged on her answer. He knew with painful certainty which of those the last aching, empty week had been for him.

"Loneliness." She spoke so quietly he almost didn't hear. That single word gave him hope. Gave him courage. If she'd been even half as lonely as he had…

Nick closed the distance between them, his steps on the wooden boards loud in the enshrining silence. He looked at her slender hands on the railing and at his own, larger and gripping almost as fiercely. The faint scent of her shampoo reached him and he closed his eyes as though that could help him fight its visceral impact.

He'd analyzed everything. Everything they'd said and done. But all the careful analysis in the world couldn't give him the answers he needed. They lay with her alone. He could hope—desperately—but he couldn't be certain.

He looked out over the distant rows of vines. "I've bought your neighbor's vineyard."

He sensed rather than saw her head jerk up. "What? Why?"

"Because you didn't want the bungalow. You wouldn't come to me." He looked at her, noted the dark smudges beneath her eyes. "You never really explained why you didn't want the bungalow."

Color leached from her already pale face. "Leave it, Nick." The words were angry and the gaping chasm at his feet widened. "It hurts too much."

He knew too well that crippling hurt. Just as he knew the terror of failure—possibly for the first time ever. His hand closed around the small box in his pocket. No other outcome had ever mattered this much. "I can't leave it. I have to know."

She turned to him then, met him with a fierce glare. "Because I won't be tucked conveniently away. I won't compromise."

"Neither will I." He wouldn't, couldn't, be relegated to a corner of her life. Alternate weekends as the father of their child. Perhaps not even seeing *her*. "I signed my share of Ivy Cottage back to you."

"I know. The documents came yesterday. Good for you. One less commitment. What I don't understand is why, with that out of the way, you're here now?" She turned away. "Shouldn't you get going? Don't you have a plane to catch? A life to live?" She bit down on her lips as she stared straight ahead, as though the existence of the world beyond depended on her not breaking her gaze.

"That's not why I did it." How had she got that so wrong? How had he? "I did it because I wanted you to have freedom."

"I know. Freedom. You were always honest about that. So—great. I've got it. Thanks." She started to turn away, to head back into the house.

"Not freedom from commitments but freedom to choose."

She paused, her back to him. "To choose what?"

"To choose your commitments."

She half turned, looked at him askance. Hurt and hope warred in her expression. He had to do it. It was the only way. All or nothing. He crossed to stand in front of her. He needed to see her eyes. Needed her to see everything that was in his. In every other facet of his life he maintained absolute control. But somehow he'd ceded control over his happiness, his future, to the woman standing in front of him. He pulled the small velvet-covered box from his pocket, held it open toward her. The diamond solitaire caught the light. "I'm asking you to marry me."

Her arms stayed by her sides. Her fists clenched. "No."

His throat tightened as he gently closed the box, slid it back into his pocket. "No?" With his thumb he wiped away the tear that slid down her cheek. It was not a happy tear. And this wasn't going at all how he wanted—needed—it to.

She took a step back, away from his touch. "I can't marry without love. Don't ask me to. Don't do that to either of us."

"I'm not asking you to. I could love enough for both of us. For all three of us."

"I…don't understand." Confusion clouded her eyes.

"You asked once if I sometimes *knew* things and I said no. But I do. I know our baby is a girl. And the first time I saw you I knew you would change my life. Irrevocably. For the better. But I denied, even to myself, that knowledge. And I've been so busy denying my feelings for you that I never stopped to take a measure of their depth. Fathomless." He reached for her hands. "I love you, Calypso. I need you. Life is too short to throw away happiness when it's there for the taking. I'm not asking you to compromise. I'm offering you everything. All I can give." He tugged her a little closer and his heart leapt as she yielded to that pull. "I want to go to bed with you every night and to wake up with you every morning."

He turned her hands over, studied the neat, straight scar at the base of her thumb. That day seemed so long ago. "Callie." Her name came out as a whisper. He looked back up, tried to read her thoughts in her eyes. A myriad of emotions flickered there, none he could be sure of.

He tucked a strand of hair behind her ear, just for the excuse of touching her further. "We talked about freedom. But real freedom comes with having choice. And I choose you. I just need you to choose me back. I love you. I want to marry you, to live with you always. You're already in my heart, already a part of me, hopelessly entangled." He waited. Watched. "Say yes, Callie." His whole being focused on that one plea.

Her silence lasted an eternity. Her eyes brimmed with tears. Please let them be happy tears. And suddenly he was terrified of her response.

She nodded, and a tear spilled from her lashes and down her cheek toward the smile that trembled on her lips. "I love you."

"Is that a yes?" He hardly dared hope.

"That's a yes." She smiled as she stepped into his arms, tilted her head up and silenced his questions the very best way possible—by taking his breath away completely.

Epilogue

Callie sat at the table beneath the vine-covered pergola and let the laughter and conversation of the Brunicadi clan wash over her. She looked at Nick, her husband, and the man of her dreams, sitting opposite her, and her attention was captured and held by the fathomless love in his river-green eyes.

"It's my turn now." Her mother, heedless of interrupting their silent communication, appeared at Nick's shoulder, her arms held out expectantly, silver bangles tinkling.

Nick gazed at Emma, two months old, cradled in his arms and still wearing the lacy antique gown each of the Brunicadi children had worn for their christenings for the last three generations. He touched a knuckle to her cheek.

Once he'd recovered from the awe of their daughter's perfection, he had taken to fatherhood with the confidence and competence with which he did everything. And with the fierce love and protectiveness Callie had predicted. He held Emma a little closer. "But she's asleep."

"It's a grandmother's right. Besides, you know she won't wake. She sleeps like…a baby." Callie's free-spirited mother could be surprisingly adamant when it came to her only grandchild. And she took sly delight in pushing any advantage she could over her new son-in-law. It was a subtle interplay they both seemed to enjoy.

Smiling down at his daughter, Nick reluctantly relinquished her, then took the opportunity to come and sit beside Callie. Beneath the table, he laced his fingers through hers and they watched as Gypsy sashayed around the gathering showing off her granddaughter to renewed *oohs* and *ahhs*. She paused beside Michael, who was flirting shamelessly—but to no visible effect—with Shannon.

Callie leaned in to Nick. "I'm so glad Shannon could come over for this. She's loving running the New Zealand office."

"You knew she would."

"And with the new designer they've taken on, they may not even need me to come back."

"We'll all always need you. Just remember, the freedom to choose is yours."

"I know." Callie turned to Melody seated beside her, before the love in Nick's eyes had her taking his hand to leave the celebration early. "How are you doing?" she asked, looking at where Mel's fingers rested over her gently pregnant belly.

"We're doing good." Mel was under the close watch of her obstetrician and had so far breezed through the pregnancy. But they were taking no chances. "Everything's progressing as it should." She leaned in a little closer. "I felt the first movements yesterday." Her smile proclaimed her joy. Mel turned that smile on Jason, as he came to stand behind her, resting his hands possessively on her shoulders, massaging gently. He bent his head between Callie and Mel. "Rosa's knitting again," he whispered as though revealing an addict's relapse. "More booties."

Nick laughed. "Rosa," he called down the table, "you have to stop knitting. There are only so many booties a baby needs."

Rosa smiled, a knowing twinkle in her dark eyes, and spoke into a lull in the conversation. "But twins need so much more."

A sudden hush fell over the table. Melody and Jason looked at one another, eyes wide and smiles even wider. "Guess that saves us deciding when to share that particular news." Mel reached up to cover Jason's hand with one of her own.

That night, as Nick and Callie stood looking down at their daughter sleeping in her crib, Callie turned to him. "Are there any more Brunicadi predictions I should know about?"

Nick touched a finger to her cheek, and his eyes darkened, even as his dimple appeared. Callie couldn't stop the bone-deep reaction that was as swift as it was powerful.

"Yes," he said as he reached for her hand. "I have a feeling it's going to be a very good night."

* * * * *

*Celebrate 60 years of pure
reading pleasure with Harlequin!*

To commemorate the event, Harlequin Intrigue® is thrilled to invite you to the wedding of The Colby Agency's J. T. Baxley and his bride, Eve Mattson.

That is, of course, if J.T. can find the woman who left him at the altar. Considering he's a private investigator for one of the top agencies in the country—the best of the best—that shouldn't be a problem. The real setback is that his bride isn't who she appears to be…and her mysterious past has put them both in danger.

*Enjoy an exclusive glimpse of
Debra Webb's latest addition to*
THE COLBY AGENCY:
ELITE RECONNAISSANCE DIVISION

THE BRIDE'S SECRETS

Available August 2009 from Harlequin Intrigue®.

The dark figures on the dock were still firing. The bullets cutting through the surface of the water without the warning boom of shots told Eve they were using silencers.

That was to her benefit. Silencers decreased the accuracy of every shot and lessened the range.

She grabbed for the rocks. Scrambled through the darkness. Bumped her knee on a boulder. Cursed.

Burrowing into the waist-deep grass, she kept low and crawled forward. Faster. Pushed harder. Needed as much distance as possible.

Shots pinged on the rocks.

J.T. scrambled alongside her.

He was breathing hard.

They had to stay close to the ground until they reached the next row of warehouses. Even though she was relatively certain they were out of range at this point, she wasn't taking any risks. And she wasn't slowing down.

J.T. had to keep up.

The splat of a bullet hitting the ground next to Eve had her rolling left. Maybe they weren't completely out of range.

She bumped J.T. He grunted.

His injured arm. Dammit. She could apologize later.

Half a dozen more yards.

Almost in the clear.

As she reached the cover of the alley between the first two warehouses she tensed.

Silence.

No pings or splats.

She glanced back at the dock. Deserted.

Time to run.

Her car was parked another block down.

Pushing to her feet, she sprinted forward. The wet bag dragged at her shoulder. She ignored it.

By the time she reached the lot where her car was parked, she had dug the keys from her pocket and hit the fob. Six seconds later she was behind the wheel. She hit the ignition as J.T. collapsed into the passenger seat. Tires squealed as she spun out of the slot.

"What the hell did you do to me?"

From the corner of her eye she watched him shake his head in an attempt to clear it.

He would be pissed when she told him about the tranquilizer.

She'd needed him cooperative until she formulated a plan. A drug-induced state of unconsciousness had been the fastest and most efficient method to ensure his continued solidarity.

"I can't really talk right now." Eve weaved into the right lane as the street widened to four lanes. What she needed was traffic. It was Saturday night—shouldn't be that difficult to find as soon as they were out of the old warehouse district.

A glance in the rearview mirror warned that their unwanted company had caught up.

Sensing her tension, J.T. turned to peer over his left shoulder.

"I hope you have a plan B."

She shot him a look. "There's always plan G." Then she pulled the Glock out of her waistband.

Cutting the steering wheel left, she slid between two vehicles. Another veer to the right and she'd put several cars between hers and the enemy.

She was betting they wouldn't pull out the firepower in the open like this, but a girl could never be too sure when it came to an unknown enemy.

Deep blending was the way to go.

Two traffic lights ahead the marquis of a movie theater provided exactly the opportunity she was looking for.

The digital numbers on the dash indicated it was just past midnight. Perfect timing. The late movie would be purging its audience into the crowd of teenagers who liked hanging out in the parking lot.

She took a hard right onto the property that sported a twelve-screen theater, numerous fast-food hot spots and a chain superstore. Speeding across the lot, she selected a lane of parking slots. Pulling in as close to the theater entrance as possible, she shut off the engine and reached for her door.

"Let's go."

Thankfully he didn't argue.

Rounding the hood of her car, she shoved the Glock into her bag, then wrapped her arm around J.T.'s and merged into the crowd.

With her free hand she finger-combed her long hair. It was soaked, as were her clothes. The kids she bumped into noticed, gave her death-ray glares.

They just didn't know.

As she and J.T. moved in closer to the building, she grabbed a baseball cap from an innocent bystander. The crowd made it easy. The kid who owned the cap had made it even easier by stuffing the cap bill-first into his waistband at the small of his back.

Pushing through the loitering crowd, she made her way to the side of the building next to the main entrance. She pushed J.T. against the wall and dropped her bag to the ground. Peeled off her tee and let it fall.

His gaze instantly zeroed in on her breasts, where the cami she wore had glued to her skin like an extra layer. A zing of desire shot through her veins.

Not the time.

With a flick of her wrist she twisted her hair up and clamped the cap atop the blonde mass.

"They're coming," J.T. muttered as he gazed at some point beyond her.

"Yeah, I know." She planted her palms against the wall on either side of him and leaned in. "Keep your eyes open. Let me know when they're inside."

Then she planted her lips on his.

* * * * *

Will J.T. and Eve be caught in the moment?
Or will Eve get the chance to reveal all of her secrets?
Find out in
THE BRIDE'S SECRETS
by Debra Webb.
Available August 2009 from Harlequin Intrigue®

You're invited to join our Tell Harlequin Reader Panel!

By joining our new reader panel you will:

- Receive Harlequin® books—they are FREE and yours to keep with no obligation to purchase anything!
- Participate in fun online surveys
- Exchange opinions and ideas with women just like you
- Have a say in our new book ideas and help us publish the best in women's fiction

In addition, you will have a chance to win great prizes and receive special gifts!
See Web site for details. Some conditions apply.
Space is limited.

To join, visit us at
www.TellHarlequin.com.

THBPA0108

REQUEST YOUR FREE BOOKS!

2 FREE NOVELS PLUS 2 FREE GIFTS!

Silhouette®

Desire®

Passionate, Powerful, Provocative!

YES! Please send me 2 FREE Silhouette Desire® novels and my 2 FREE gifts (gifts are worth about $10). After receiving them, if I don't wish to receive any more books, I can return the shipping statement marked "cancel". If I don't cancel, I will receive 6 brand-new novels every month and be billed just $4.05 per book in the U.S. or $4.74 per book in Canada. That's a savings of almost 15% off the cover price! It's quite a bargain! Shipping and handling is just 50¢ per book.* I understand that accepting the 2 free books and gifts places me under no obligation to buy anything. I can always return a shipment and cancel at any time. Even if I never buy another book, the two free books and gifts are mine to keep forever.

225 SDN EYMS 326 SDN EYM4

Name _____ (PLEASE PRINT)

Address _____ Apt. #

City _____ State/Prov. _____ Zip/Postal Code

Signature (if under 18, a parent or guardian must sign)

Mail to the **Silhouette Reader Service:**
IN U.S.A.: P.O. Box 1867, Buffalo, NY 14240-1867
IN CANADA: P.O. Box 609, Fort Erie, Ontario L2A 5X3

Not valid to current subscribers of Silhouette Desire books.

Want to try two free books from another line?
Call 1-800-873-8635 or visit www.morefreebooks.com.

* Terms and prices subject to change without notice. Prices do not include applicable taxes. Sales tax applicable in N.Y. Canadian residents will be charged applicable provincial taxes and GST. Offer not valid in Quebec. This offer is limited to one order per household. All orders subject to approval. Credit or debit balances in a customer's account(s) may be offset by any other outstanding balance owed by or to the customer. Please allow 4 to 6 weeks for delivery. Offer available while quantities last.

Your Privacy: Silhouette Books is committed to protecting your privacy. Our Privacy Policy is available online at www.eHarlequin.com or upon request from the Reader Service. From time to time we make our lists of customers available to reputable third parties who have a product or service of interest to you. If you would prefer we not share your name and address, please check here. ☐

SDES09R

Stay up-to-date on all your romance reading news!

The Harlequin Inside Romance newsletter is a **FREE** quarterly newsletter highlighting our upcoming series releases and promotions!

Go to
eHarlequin.com/InsideRomance
or e-mail us at
InsideRomance@Harlequin.com
to sign up to receive
your **FREE** newsletter today!

HARLEQUIN® *Romance*®

Welcome to the intensely emotional world of

MARGARET WAY

with

Cattle Baron: Nanny Needed

It's a media scandal! Flame-haired beauty
Amber Wyatt has gate-crashed her ex-fiancé's
glamorous society wedding. Groomsman
Cal McFarlane knows she's trouble, but when
Amber loses her job, the rugged cattle rancher
comes to the rescue. He needs a nanny, and
if it makes his baby nephew happy, he's
willing to play with fire....

*Available in August
wherever books are sold.*